Heineman

Four

The World Around Us

Heinemann Short Stories
Four

The World Around Us

Selected and edited by Rhodri Jones
Headmaster of John Kelly Boys' High School, Brent

Heinemann Educational Books
LONDON

Heinemann Educational Books Ltd
22 Bedford Square, London WC1B 3HH
LONDON   EDINBURGH   MELBOURNE   AUCKLAND
HONG KONG   SINGAPORE   KUALA LUMPUR   NEW DELHI
IBADAN   NAIROBI   JOHANNESBURG
EXETER (NH)   KINGSTON   PORT OF SPAIN

Selection, Introduction and Follow On © Rhodri Jones 1980

Cover design and photography by Chris Gilbert

First published 1980
Reprinted 1981

British Library Cataloguing in Publication Data

Heinemann short stories.
   Book 4: The world around us
   1. Short stories, English
   I. Jones, Rhodri
   823'.9'1FS   PR1309.S5

   ISBN 0–435–13493–0

Printed and bound in Hong Kong by
Dah Hua Company Ltd

Contents

Acknowledgements

The editor and publishers wish to thank the following for permission to reproduce copyright material:
Hart-Davis MacGibbon and A. D. Peters for 'A Minority' from *Collection Three* by Frank O'Connor, and for 'The Other Foot' from *The Illustrated Man* by Ray Bradbury; A. M. Heath & Co for 'Stop Thief!' from *A Long Way from London* by Dan Jacobson, and for 'Wine on the Desert' from *Max Brand's Best Stories* by Max Brand; Laurence Pollinger for 'The Destructors' from *Collected Stories of Graham Greene* by Graham Greene; Michael Joseph and Penguin Books for 'Lamb to the Slaughter' from *Someone Like You* by Roald Dahl; Curtis Brown, London for 'A Mild Attack of Locusts' from *The Sun Between Their Feet* by Doris Lessing; C. & J. Wolfers for 'The Drowned Giant' by J. G. Ballard © 1964 by J. G. Ballard taken from *The Terminal Beach*, Penguin Books, London; Brian W. Aldiss and Faber & Faber for 'Who Can Replace a Man?' from *The Best Science Fiction Stories of Brian W. Aldiss* by Brian W. Aldiss.

Illustrations

Introduction

The short stories in this collection are intended primarily to be read for entertainment and pleasure. They should appeal particularly to pupils in the fourth (or fifth) year of the secondary school.

All the stories in their different ways reflect aspects of the world that are around us today – the scourge of intolerance, the problem of violence, the struggle man has with his environment. Even the stories which seem to be examples of science fiction cast a light on the world that is around us now. By reading these stories, you may gain a deeper understanding of these areas of experience.

You can also learn more about the skill of the story-tellers contained here and may be able to adapt what you learn about their technique to the stories you write yourself. To help you, there are notes and suggestions for discussion and writing on each story at the end of the volume. There are also suggestions for further books by the writers selected here so that you can go on to read more of their stories and novels.

A Minority

FRANK O'CONNOR

Denis Halligan noticed Willy Stein for the first time one Sunday when the other fellows were at Mass. As Denis was a Protestant, he didn't go to Mass. Instead, he sat on the steps outside the chapel with Willy. Willy was a thin, seedy little chap with long, wild hair. It was an autumn morning; there was mist on the trees, and you could scarcely see the great ring of mountains that cut them off there in the middle of Ireland, miles from anywhere.

'Why did they send you here if you're a Proddy?' asked Willy.

'I don't know,' said Denis, who felt his background was so queer that he didn't want to explain it to anybody. 'I suppose because it was cheap.'

'Is your old fellow a Catholic?' asked Willy.

'No,' replied Denis. 'Is yours?'

'No,' Willy said contemptuously. 'He was a Proddy. My old one was a Proddy, too.'

'Where do they live?' asked Denis.

'They're dead,' Willey said, making the motion of spitting. 'The bloody Germans killed them.'

'Oh, cripes!' Denis said regretfully. Denis had a great admiration for everything German, particularly tank generals, and when he grew up he wanted to be a tank general himself, but it seemed a pity that they had to kill Willy's father and mother. Bad as it was to have your parents separated, as his own were, it was worse having them dead. 'Was it a bomb?' he asked.

'No,' Willy replied without undue emotion. 'They were killed in a camp. They sent me over to the Cumminses in Dublin or I'd have been killed too. The Cumminses are Catholics. That's why I was sent here.'

'Do you like it here?' asked Denis.

'I do not,' Willy said scornfully in his slummy Dublin accent, and then took out a slingshot and fitted a stone in it.

3

'I'd sooner Vienna. Vienna was gas. When I grow up I'm going to get out of this blooming place.'

'But what will you do?'

'Aw, go to sea, or something. I don't care.'

Denis was interested in Willy. Apart from the fact that they were the only Proddies in the school, Willy struck him as being really tough, and Denis admired toughness. He was always trying to be tough himself, but there was a soft streak in him that kept breaking out. It was breaking out now, and he knew it. Though he saw that Willy didn't give a rap about his parents, Denis couldn't help being sorry for him, alone in the middle of Ireland with his father and mother dead half a world away. He said as much to his friend Nigel Healy, from Cork, that afternoon, but Nigel only gave a superior sniff.

'But that fellow is mad,' he said, in his reasonable way.

'How is he mad?' asked Denis.

'He's not even left go home on holidays,' explained Nigel. 'He has to stay here all during the summer. Those people were nice to him, and what does he do? Breaks every window in the place. They had the police to the house twice. He's mad on slingshots.'

'He had one this morning,' said Denis.

'Last time he was caught with one he got flogged,' said Nigel. 'You see, the fellow has no sense. I even saw him putting sugar on his meat.'

'But why did he do that?' asked Denis.

'Said he liked it,' replied Nigel with a smile and a shrug. 'He's bound to get expelled one of these days. You'd want to mind yourself with him.'

But for some reason that only made Denis more interested in Willy Stein, and he looked forward to meeting him again by himself the following Sunday. He was curious to know why the Germans would want to kill Stein's father and mother. That seemed to him a funny thing to do – unless, of course, they were spies for the English.

Again they sat on the steps, but this morning the sun was warm and bright, and the mountains all round them were a brilliant blue. If Stein's parents were really spies, the idea of it did not seem to have occurred to him. According to him, his father had been a lawyer and his mother something on a newspaper, and he didn't seem to remember much about them

4

except that they were both 'gas'. Everything with Stein was 'gas'. His mother was gentle and timid, and let him have everything he wanted, so she was 'great gas'. His father was sure she was ruining him, and was always on to him to study and be better than other kids, and when his father got like that he used to weep and shout and wave his hands, but that was only now and then. He was gas, too, though not, Denis gathered, great gas. Willy suddenly waved his hands and shouted something in a foreign language.

'What's that?' asked Denis with the deepest admiration.

'German,' Stein replied, in his graceless way.

'What does it mean?' asked Denis.

'I dunno,' Stein said lightly.

Denis was disappointed. For a fellow like himself, who was interested in tanks, a spatter of German might one day be useful. He had the impression that Stein was only letting on to remember parents he had lost before he was really old enough to remember them.

Their talk was interrupted by Father Houlihan, a tall, morose-looking priest. He had a bad belly and a worse temper, but Denis knew Father Houlihan liked him, and he admired Father Houlihan. He was violent, but he wasn't a stinker.

'Hah!' he said, in his mocking way. 'And what do you two cock sparrows think you're doing out here?'

'We're excused, Father,' Denis said brightly, leaping to his feet.

'No one is excused anything in this place till I excuse him,' snarled Father Houlihan cheerfully, 'and I don't excuse much. Run into Mass now, ye pair of heathens!'

'But we're Protestants, Father!' Stein cried, and Denis was half afraid of seeing the red flush on Father Houlihan's forehead that showed he was out for blood.

'Aha, what fine Protestants we have in ye!' he snorted good-humouredly. 'I suppose you have a Protestant slingshot in your pocket at this very minute, you scoundrel, you!'

'I have not!' Stein shouted. 'You know Murphy took it off me.'

'Mr Murphy to you, Willy Stein,' said the priest, pinching his ear playfully and pushing him towards the chapel. 'And next time I catch you with a slingshot I'll give you a Catholic cane on your fat Protestant backside.'

The two boys went into chapel and sat together on a bench at the back. Willy was muttering indignantly to himself, but he waited until everyone was kneeling with bowed head. Then, to Denis's horror, he took out a slingshot and a bit of paper, which he chewed up into a wet ball. There was nothing hasty or spontaneous about this. Stein went about it with a concentration that was almost pious. As the bell rang for the Consecration, there was a *ping*, and a seminarist kneeling at the side of the chapel put his hand to his ear and looked angrily round. But by this time Stein had thrown himself on his knees, and his eyes were shut in a look of rapt devotion. It gave Denis quite a turn. Even if he wasn't a Catholic, he had been brought up to respect every form of religon.

The business of going to Mass and feeling out of it made Denis Halligan completely fed up with being a Proddy. He had never liked it anyway, even at home, as a kid. He was gregarious, and a born gang leader, a promoter of organisation, and it cut him to the heart to feel that at any moment he might be deserted by his gang because, through no fault of his own, he was not a Catholic and might accidentally say or do the wrong thing. He even resented the quiet persuasion that the school authorities exercised on him. A senior called Hanley, whom Nigel described sarcastically as 'Halligan's angel', was attached to Denis – not to proselytise, but to give him an intelligent understanding of the religious life of the group. Hanley had previously been attached to Stein, but that had proved hopeless, because Stein seemed to take Hanley's company as a guarantee of immunity from punishment, so he merely involved Hanley in every form of forbidden activity, from smoking to stealing. One day when Stein stole a gold tie-pin from a master's room, Hanley had to report him. On Hanley's account, he was not flogged, but told to put the tie-pin back in the place from which he had taken it. Stein did so, and seized the opportunity to pinch five shillings instead, and this theft was discovered only when someone saw Stein fast asleep in bed with his mouth open and the two half-crowns in his jaw. As Hanley, a sweet and saintly boy, said to Denis, it wasn't Stein's fault. He was just unbalanced.

In any other circumstances Denis would have enjoyed Hanley's attention, but it made him mad to be singled out like this and looked after like some kid who couldn't undo his own buttons.

'Listen, Hanley,' he said angrily one day when he and Nigel were discussing football and Hanley had slipped a little homily into the conversation. 'It's no good preaching at me. It's not my fault that I'm a Proddy.'

'Well, you don't have to be a Proddy if you don't want to be,' Hanley said with a smile. 'Do you?'

'How can I help it?' asked Denis.

'Well, who'd stop you?'

'My mother would, for one.'

'Did you try?'

'What do you mean, Hanley?'

'I mean, why don't you ask her?' Hanley went on, in the same bland way. 'I wouldn't be too sure she wants you to be a Proddy.'

'How could I ask her?'

'You could write. Or phone,' Hanley added hastily, seeing the look on Denis's face at the notion of writing an extra letter. 'Father Houlihan would let you use the telephone, if you asked him. Or I'll ask him, if you like.'

'Do if you want to,' said Denis. 'I don't care.'

He didn't really believe his mother would agree to something he wanted, just like that, but he had no objection to a free telephone call that would enable him to hear her voice again. To his astonishment, she made no difficulty about it.

'Why, of course, darling,' she said sweetly. 'If that's how you feel and Father Houlihan has no objection, I don't mind. You know I only want you to be happy at school.'

It was a colossal relief. Overnight, his whole position in the school changed. He had ceased to be an outsider. He was one of the gang. He might even be Chief Gang Leader in the course of time. He was a warm-hearted boy, and he had the feeling that by a simple gesture he had conferred an immense benefit on everybody. The only person who didn't seem too enthusiastic was Father Houlihan, but then he was not much of an enthusiast anyway. 'My bold young convert,' he said, pulling Denis's ear, 'I suppose any day now you'll start paying attention to your lessons.'

Yet the moment he had made his decision, he began to feel guilty about young Stein. As has been said, he was not only gregarious, but he was also a born gang leader, and had the feeling that someone might think he had deserted an ally to

7

secure his own advantage. He was suddenly filled with a wild desire to convert Willy as well, so that the pair of them could be received as a group. He saw it as even more of a duty of Willy's than of his own. Willy had been saved from his parents' fate by a good kind Catholic family, and it was the least they could expect that Willy should show his gratitude to them, to the school, and to Ireland.

But Willy seemed to have a deplorable head for theology. All the time they talked Denis had the impression that Willy was only planning some fresh mischief.

'Ah, come on, Willy,' he said authoritatively, 'you don't want to be a blooming old Proddy.'

'I don't want to be a Cat either,' said Willy with a shrug.

'Don't you want to be like the other fellows in the school?'

'Why don't they want to be like me?' asked Stein.

'Because there's only two of us, and there's hundreds of them. And they're right.'

'And if there were hundreds of us and two of them, we'd be right, I suppose?' Stein said with a sneer. 'You want to be like the rest of them. All right, be like the rest of them, but let me alone.'

'I'm only speaking for your own good,' Denis said, getting mad. What really made him mad was the feeling that somehow Stein wasn't speaking to him at all; that inside, he was as lonely and lost as Denis would have been in similar circumstances, and he wouldn't admit to it, wouldn't break down as Denis would have done. What he really wanted to do was to give Stein a sock in the gob, but he knew that even this was no good. Stein was always being beaten, and he always yelled bloody murder, and next day he came back and did the same thing again. Everyone was thinking exclusively of Stein's good, and it always ended up by their beating him, and it never did him any good at all.

Denis confided his difficulties to Hanley, who was also full of concern for Stein's good, but Hanley only smiled sadly and shook his head.

'I know more about that than you do, Denis,' he said, in his fatherly way. 'I'll tell you if you promise not to repeat it to a living soul.'

'What is it?' asked Denis eagerly.

'Promise! Mind, this is serious!'

8

'Oh, I promise.'

'The fact is that Stein isn't a Proddy at all,' Hanley said sadly.

'But what is he?'

'Stein is a Jew,' Hanley said in a low voice. 'That's why his father and mother were killed. Nobody knows that, though.'

'But does Stein know he's a Jew?' Denis asked excitedly.

'No. And mind, we're not supposed to know it, either. Nobody knows it, except the priests and ourselves.'

'But why doesn't somebody tell him?'

'Because if they did, he might blab about it – you know, he's not very smart – and then all the fellows would be jeering at him. Remember, Denis, if you ever mentioned it, Father Houlihan would skin you alive. He says Stein is after suffering enough. He's sorry for Stein. Mind, I'm only warning you.'

'But won't it be awful for him when he finds out?'

'When he's older and has a job, he won't mind it so much,' said Hanley.

But Denis wasn't sure. Somehow, he had an idea that Stein wanted to stay a Proddy simply because that was what his father and mother had been and it was now the only link he had with them, and if someone would just tell him, he wouldn't care so much and would probably become a Catholic, like Denis. Afterwards, when he did find out that everything he had done was mistaken, it might be too late. And this – and the fact that Father Houlihan, whom Denis admired, was also sorry for Willy Stein – increased his feeling of guilt, and he almost wished he hadn't been in such a hurry himself about being converted. Denis wasn't a bright student, but he was a born officer and he would never have deserted his men.

The excitement of his own reception into the Church almost banished the thought of Stein from his mind. On the Sunday he was received he was allowed to sleep late, and Murphy, the seminarist, even brought him comics to read in bed. This was real style! Then he dressed in his best suit and went down to meet his mother, who arrived, with his sister, Martha, in a hired car. For once, Martha was deferential. She was impressed, and the sight of the chapel impressed her even more. In front of the High Altar there was an isolated prie-dieu for Denis himself, and behind him a special pew was reserved for her and his mother.

Denis knew afterwards that he hadn't made a single false move. Only once was his exaltation disturbed, and that was when he heard the *ping* of a slingshot and realised that Stein, sitting by himself in the back row, was whiling away the time by getting into fresh mischief. The rage rose up in Denis, in spite of all his holy thoughts, and for a moment he resolved that when it was all over he would find Willy Stein and beat him to a jelly.

Instead, when it was over he suddenly felt weary. Martha had ceased to be impressed by him. Now she was just a sister a bare year younger who was mad with him for having stolen the attention of everybody. She knew only too well what a figure she would have cut as a convert, and was crazy with jealousy.

'I won't stand it,' she said. 'I'm going to be a Catholic, too.'

'Well, who's stopping you?' Denis asked.

'Nobody's going to stop me,' said Martha. 'Just because Daddy is fond of you doesn't mean that I can't be a Catholic.'

'What has Daddy to do with it?' asked Denis with a feeling of alarm.

'Because now that you're a Catholic, the courts wouldn't let him have you,' Martha said excitedly. 'Because Daddy is an atheist, or something, and he wanted to get hold of you. He tried to get you away from Mummy. I don't care about Daddy. I'm going to be converted, too.'

'Go on!' growled Denis, feeling sadly how his mood of exaltation was fading. 'You're only an old copycat.'

'I am not a copycat, Denis Halligan,' she said bitterly, 'It's only that you always sucked up to Daddy and I didn't, and he doesn't care about me. I don't care about him, either, so there!'

Denis felt a sudden pang of terror at her words. In a dim sort of way he realized that what he had done might have consequences he had never contemplated. He had no wish to live with his father, but his father came to the school to see him sometimes, and he had always had the feeling that if he ever got fed up with living at home with his mother and Martha, his father would always have him. Nobody had told him that by becoming a Catholic he had made it impossible for his father to have him. He glanced round and saw Stein, thin and pale and furtive, slouching away from the chapel with his hand in his pocket clutching his slingshot. He gave Denis a grin in which there was no malice, but Denis scowled and looked away.

10

'Who's that?' asked Martha inquisitively.

'Oh him!' Denis said contemptuously. 'That's only a dirty Jew-boy.'

Yet even as he spoke the words he knew they were false. What he really felt towards Willy Stein was an aching envy. Nobody had told him that by changing his faith he might be unfaithful to his father, but nobody had told Stein, either, and, alone and despairing, he still clung to a faith that was not his own for the sake of a father and mother he had already almost forgotten, who had been murdered half a world away and whom he would never see again. For a single moment Denis saw the dirty little delinquent whom everyone pitied and despised transfigured by a glory that he himself would never know.

Stop Thief!

DAN JACOBSON

A black-browed angry-looking man he was, and the games he played with his children were always angry games; he was chasing them, he was growling at them, he was snapping his teeth at them, while they shrieked with delight and fear, going pale and tense with fear, but coming back for more, and hanging on to his hands when he declared that he had had enough. There was a boy and a girl, both dark-haired and thin, the boy a little older than his sister and protective towards her with servants and strangers, with everyone but his father: he did not dare to protect her when his father sprang at her from behind a bush, and carried her shrieking, upside down, to his lair that was, he told them, littered with the bones of other children that he had already eaten.

The mother sat aside from these games – she sat at the tea table at the head of the small sweep of lawn towards the swimming bath, beyond which were the trees where her husband and children played, or she lay in the sun on the side of the swimming bath, with a towel about her head, and it was only rarely that she called to them or warned them of their father's stealthy, mock approaches. She sun-bathed or she read in the sun; they were all sun-tanned in that family, from spending so much time at their swimming bath, and from their annual six-weeks' holiday at the Cape, where they lived the life simple in a seaside cottage with only one servant. The big house in Johannesburg seemed to have innumerable servants, all black men in gleaming white jackets and aprons and little white caps like those of an Indian political movement, but in fact only another sign of their servitude, and these black men kept the house like a house on show: the house shone, unmarked by the pressures, the stains and splashes, the disorder of living. Not that the children were the least bit tidy – they dropped things about them as they went, and left the toys and the sticks and the items of clothing lying where they had been dropped, but the servants followed picking up things and putting them in drawers, as though that was all that they had been born for, this dance of attendance on the two nervous dark-haired children. And the mother, who had been poorly brought up, loved it in the children that they had, so without question or wonder, the insolence of wealth. Once when he had hardly been more than a baby she had asked the boy: 'Would you like to be a little black boy?'

The child had been puzzled that his mother should have asked this. 'No,' he said, frowning, bringing his dark eyebrows together, and looking up in puzzled distaste.

'Why not?'

The puzzlement had left the boy's face, and there had been only distaste as he replied, 'They have nasty clothes.' And for this he had been given a kiss, which he accepted demurely. The children accepted their mother's affection as a matter of course; it was for their father's mock-anger that they lived. The mother knew this and did not resent it: she believed that the insolence she loved in them had come from their father, and for her her husband's violence was profoundly confused with his wealth.

But sometimes, watching the children at their perilous play with their father, even the mother would be afraid. She would lift her eyes from her book, or unwrap the towel which had been muffling the sun's rays to a yellow blur on her eyes, and her heart would sink with fear to see them run and stand breathing behind some tree while their father prowled on tiptoe towards them. So frail they seemed, with their bony elbows poking out from their short-sleeved blouses, and their knees large and round below the dress or khaki shorts that each wore. And he seemed so determined, so muscular in the casual clothing he wore in the evenings, after he had come from work, so large above the children. But she accepted his violence and his strength, and she never protested against the games. She would sometimes watch them play, but her eyes would go back to the book, or she would again carefully wrap the towel about her eyes and her ears, and sink back into her drowse. She seemed sunken under her husband, under his wealth, under his strength; they had come down upon her as the sun did where she lay at the side of the swimming bath, and she questioned them no more than she could have questioned the sun. She had submitted to them.

The father laughed, showing his white teeth, when the

children ran yelling from him. In the shadows of the trees they waited for him to come again. He moved slowly towards them, and a lift of his arm made them scamper. He was king of his castle – and castle enough the house was too, in its several acres of ground, and its trees that cut it off from sight of the road.

Then one night the burglar came to their house. It was not for nothing that their house, like every other house in Johannesburg, had every window barred with steel burglar-proofing, that every door had a double lock, that two large dogs were let loose in the grounds at night. It was not for nothing that the father had a revolver in his wardrobe, always loaded and on a high shelf out of reach from the children. For the burglars in Johannesburg can be an ugly lot – gangsters, marauders, hard black men who seem to have nothing to lose, who carry with them knives and knuckledusters and guns.

But this one was not one of these. This one was a boy, a fool, a beginner, come by himself to the wrong house, barked at by the dogs where he stood in the darkness of a corner of the garage between the large painted mudguard of a car and a workbench behind him. He did not even reach for one of the chisels on the bench behind him, but stood squeezing the fingers of one hand in the grasp of the other, as though by that alone he might be able to stop the shivering which shook his shoulders in quick, awful spasms.

But the house did not know what he was and what he might do. The whole house was wild with lights and shouts and the banging of doors. Men, women, they had tumbled out pell-mell from the rooms in which they slept; one of the servants had been roused by the barking of dogs and had seen the burglar slipping into the garage. The house had all been in darkness, and still, so still that not even the trees had moved under the brilliance of the stars in the early morning sky, when the shouts of the servant had first come calamitously upon it. Wild, hoarse, archaic, the shouts had sounded, like the shouts a dreamer might dream he is making, in his deep terror of the darkness around him. Then there had been the other shouts, the house in uproar.

And the father in his pyjamas and dressing gown, with the revolver thrust unsteadily before him, was advancing across the back yard. The servants fell in behind him, even the one who had been guarding the window of the garage. 'Get to the window, you fool!' the father shouted. 'Guard the window!' Unwillingly, one or two went to the window, while the father came closer to the garage door.

He did not know what might be behind the door; he found that he could not push the garage door open, for fear the burglar might spring at him. He was a stranger to himself, roused out of bed by hoarse shouts, hurried downstairs by danger, chilled by the early morning air: to him it seemed that he had never before seen the place he was in; never before felt the lock under his hand; and when he looked back, the house, with the light falling on the paved yard from the open kitchen door, was the house of a stranger, not his at all. The servants were simply people, a throng, some carrying improvised clubs in their hands, all half-dressed, none of them known.

He could not push the door open. The dread of opening himself to whatever might be there was too great. The servants pushed a little closer; and he felt his fear growing tighter and closer within him. They pressed so closely upon him his fear had no room to move, and when he did at last lift up the revolver it was in desperation to drive away the people, who were constricting his fear and pressing it upon him. He lifted the revolver and shouted, 'Leave me!' He tilted it towards the stars and fired. The clamour of the shot was more loud and gross in his ears than he could have imagined, and with it there sprang from the muzzle a gout of flame, vivid in the darkness. When the servants shrank back he felt a momentary sense of release and relaxation, as though he had done the thing for which he had been dragged out of bed, and could be left now to go in peace. Then he felt the door behind him budge.

He leaped away from the door so violently that he stumbled and fell, and he was on his knees with the revolver scratching uselessly against the paving when the burglar came out of the garage. The servants too had staggered back when their master had leaped towards them, so the burglar stood alone in the doorway, with his hands still squeezed together, but lifted now to his chest, like someone beseeching mercy. From where he sprawled on the ground the master could only gasp: 'Catch him. Get round him!' And one or two of the men-servants came forward. They hesitated, and then they saw the spasms shaking the burglar, so they came to him and took him roughly, pinioning him. Their master was struggling to his feet.

'Bring him into the kitchen,' he said. There was a sigh from the group of servants, and a babble, then eagerly they began jostling the burglar towards the kitchen, and he went unresistingly.

To the father the kitchen too looked harsh and strange, a place of urgency, and there seemed to be too many people in it: all the servants, and his wife, and the two children, and the burglar, and the servants' friends, those who had been sleeping illegally but without harmful intent in the rooms in the back yard. These shrank back now, as if only now realizing that the events of the night might have consequences for themselves too, and not only for the burglar they had helped to catch.

'You've phoned the police?' the father asked.

'Yes,' the mother said. 'The flying squad's coming.'

The father sat down at the kitchen table, blowing his cheeks out with exhaustion, feeling the tension beginning to ebb from the pit of his stomach. He could not look at the burglar. The mother too, for different reasons, avoided looking at the burglar, but the two children, in their neat white pyjama suits, had eyes for nothing else. They knew all about burglars: they had grown up in Johannesburg, and they knew why the steel bars lay across their bedroom windows, and why they were not allowed outside the house after nightfall, and why the dogs roamed loose at night. But this was the first burglar they had seen. Even the revolver loose in their father's hand could not draw their eyes from the burglar.

He stood in the middle of the kitchen, and his dark eyes were dazed, unseeing. He was a young African – he looked no more than seventeen – an undersized, townbred seventeen years of age. He was wearing a soiled grey sports coat and a pair of ragged trousers that reached only about half-way down his shins, and when the spasms came he shook from his shoes upwards, even his strained brown ankles shaking, his knees, his loins, his shoulders, his head, all shaking. Then the fit would pass and he would simply stand, supported on each side by the household servants.

He seemed to see nothing, to look at nothing, to hear nothing: there seemed to be within him a secret war between his will and the spasms of shaking that came upon him, like a fit. The colour of his face was terrible: he was grey, an ash-

16

grey, a grey like that of the first thinning of the darkness after a rain-sodden night. Sometimes when every other part of his body was free of the spasm, his mouth would still be shaking; his lips were closed, but they shook, as if there were a turbulence in his mouth that he had to void. Then that too would pass.

The little boy at last looked away from the burglar to his father, and saw him sitting weakly in the chair, exhausted. The hand that held the revolver lay laxly on the kitchen table, and from it there rose a faint acrid scent, but the gun looked in his hand like a toy. The father could not move and he could not speak, he sat collapsed, until even the servants looked curiously at him, as the little boy had done, from the burglar to him, and then back to the burglar again. They murmured a little, uncertainly; the two who were holding the burglar loosened their grip on him and shuffled their feet. They waited for direction from their master, but no direction came. The little boy waited for action from his father, but no action came. The son was the first to see that his father could make no action, could give no word.

So he gave the word himself. In a voice that was barely recognizable as his own, his face with its little point of a nose contorted, he screamed in rage and disappointment: 'Hit the burglar! Hit the burglar!' He danced on his bare feet, waving his small fists in the air. 'Why don't you hit the burglar? You must hit the burglar.' He danced like a little demon in his light pyjamas. 'Hit!' he screamed. 'Hit!' His little sister joined in because she heard her brother shouting, and she added her high yell to his: 'Hit the burglar!'

'Get the children out of here!' the father shouted. The children had raised their voices for a moment only, but it had seemed endless, their little voices shrilling for blood. 'What are they doing here?' the father shouted in a fury at the mother, pulling himself up at last. 'Get them out of here!' But he made no move to help the mother, though he saw that she could not manage both dancing, capering children. And when the little boy saw that his father did not move towards him, again he screamed, 'Hit the burglar!'

'Jerry,' the mother gasped to one of the servants, 'help me. Don't stand there!' She was grappling at arm's length with the flailing hands of the little girl.

17

The dark body of the servant bent over the boy. Then he sprang back waving his hand. The boy had bitten him. So he too being near-distraught with excitement and this last unexpected little assault, reached out and hit the little boy across the back of the head. The boy staggered; he fell down and lay on the sparkling kitchen floor. But it was only for a moment. He came up growling, with hands lifted, curled inwards, and fell upon the burglar. It took two servants to prise him off, and when he was finally carried away over the black powerful shoulder of the one, he had left two deep scratches on the face of the burglar, both from the forehead down, broken by the shelf of bone over the eyes, and continued down the cheeks. The burglar had made no effort to defend himself, knowing what would happen to him if he did anything to hurt the child.

Then the police came and took the burglar away. By that time the children were safe and quiet in the nursery; and later the mother too fell asleep after taking a sedative.

But the servant who had hit the boy was dismissed the very next day, by the mother, who could not bear it that a servant should have struck a child of hers. Least of all the son to whom she now submitted, the son who after the night the burglar had come to the house was not afraid to protect his sister, when her father fell upon her in their games in the garden, and who fought, when he himself was picked up and carried away, as an adult might fight, with his fists and his feet and his knees, to hurt. His will was stronger than his father's, and soon they were facing each other like two men, and the wild games and the shrieking among the trees grew rarer. For the father was afraid of the games he sometimes still had to play with his son, and there was none among them who did not know it, neither the son, nor the daughter, nor the mother, nor the father from whose hands in one night the violence in the family had passed.

The Other Foot

RAY BRADBURY

When they heard the news they came out of the restaurants and cafés and hotels and looked at the sky. They lifted their dark hands over their upturned white eyes. Their mouths hung wide. In the hot noon for thousands of miles there were little towns where the dark people stood with their shadows under them, looking up.

In her kitchen Hattie Johnson covered the boiling soup, wiped her thin fingers on a cloth, and walked carefully to the back porch.

'Come on, Ma! Hey, Ma, come on – you'll miss it!'

'Hey, Mom!'

Three little Negro boys danced around in the dusty yard, yelling. Now and then they looked at the house frantically.

'I'm coming,' said Hattie, and opened the screen door. 'Where you hear this rumour?'

'Up at Jones's, Ma. They say a rocket's coming, first one in twenty years, with a white man in it!'

'What's a white man? I never seen one.'

'You'll find out,' said Hattie. 'Yes indeed, you'll find out.'

'Tell us about one, Ma. Tell like you did.'

Hattie frowned. 'Well, it's been a long time. I was a little girl, you see. That was back in 1965.'

'Tell us about a white man, Mom!'

She came and stood in the yard, looking up at the blue clear Martian sky with the thin white Martian clouds, and in the distance the Martian hills broiling in the heat. She said at last, 'Well, first of all, they got white hands.'

'White hands!' The boys joked, slapping each other.

'And they got white arms.'

'White arms!' hooted the boys.

'And white faces.'

'White faces! *Really*?'

'White like *this*, Mom? The smallest threw dust on his face, sneezing. 'This way?'

19

'Whiter than that,' she said gravely, and turned to the sky again. There was a troubled thing in her eyes, as if she was looking for a thunder shower up high, and not seeing it made her worry. 'Maybe you better go inside.'

'Oh, Mom!' They stared at her in disbelief. 'We got to watch, we just got to. Nothing's going to happen, is it?'

'I don't know. I got a feeling, is all.'

'We just want to see the ship and maybe run down to the port and see that white man. What's he like, huh, Mom?'

'I don't know. I just don't know,' she mused, shaking her head.

'Tell us some more!'

'Well, the white people live on Earth, which is where we all come from, twenty years ago. We just up and walked away and came to Mars and set down and built towns and here we are. Now we're Martians instead of Earth people. And no white men've come up here in all that time. That's the story.'

'Why didn't they come up, Mom?'

'Well, 'cause. Right after we got up here, Earth got in an atom war. They blew each other up terribly. They forgot us. When they finished fighting, after years, they didn't have any rockets. Took them until recently to build more. So here they come now, twenty years later, to visit.' She gazed at her children numbly and then began to walk. 'You wait here. I'm going down the line to Elizabeth Brown's house. You promise to stay?'

'We don't want to but we will.'

'All right, then.' And she ran off down the road.

At the Browns' she arrived in time to see everybody packed into the family car. 'Hey there, Hattie! Come on along!'

'Where you going?' she said, breathlessly running up.

'To see the white man!'

'That's right,' said Mr Brown seriously. He waved at his load. 'These children never saw one, and *I* almost forgot.'

'What you going to do with that white man?' asked Hattie.

'Do?' said everyone. 'Why – just *look* at him, is all.'

'You sure?'

'What else *can* we do?'

'I don't know,' said Hattie. 'I just thought there might be trouble.'

'What kind of trouble?'

'You *know*,' said Hattie vaguely, embarrassed. 'You ain't going to lynch him?'

'Lynch him?' Everyone laughed. Mr Brown slapped his knee. 'Why bless you, child, no! We're going to shake his hand. Ain't we, everyone?'

'Sure, sure!'

Another car drove up from another direction and Hattie gave a cry. 'Willie!'

'What you doing 'way down here? Where're the kids?' shouted her husband angrily. He glared at the others. 'You going down like a bunch of fools to see that man come in?'

'That appears to be just right,' agreed Mr Brown, nodding and smiling.

'Well, take your guns along,' said Willie. 'I'm on my way home for mine right now!'

'Willie!'

'You get in this car, Hattie.' He held the door open firmly, looking at her until she obeyed. Without another word to the others he roared the car down the dusty road.

'Willie, not so fast!'

'Not so fast, huh? We'll see about that.' He watched the road tear under the car. 'What right they got coming up here this late? Why don't they leave us in peace? Why didn't they blow themselves up on that old world and let us be?'

'Willie, that ain't no Christian way to talk.'

'I'm not feeling Christian,' he said savagely, gripping the wheel, 'I'm just feeling mean. After all them years of doing what they did to our folks – my mom and dad, and your mom and dad – You remember? You remember how they hung my father on Knockwood Hill and shot my mother? You remember? Or you got a memory that's short like the others?'

'I remember,' she said.

'You remember Dr Phillips and Mr Burton and their big houses, and my mother's washing shack, and Dad working when he was old, and the thanks he got was being hung by Dr Phillips and Mr Burton. Well,' said Willie, 'the shoe's on the other foot now. We'll see who gets laws passed against him, who gets lynched, who rides the back of streetcars, who gets segregated in shows. We'll just wait and see.'

'Oh, Willie, you're talking trouble.'

'Everybody's talking. Everybody's thought on this day,

21

thinking it'd never be. Thinking, What kind of day would it be if the white man ever came up here to Mars? But here's the day, and we can't run away.'

'Ain't you going to let the white people live up here?'

'Sure.' He smiled, but it was a wide, mean smile, and his eyes were mad. 'They can come up and live and work here; why, certainly. All they got to do to deserve it is live in their own small part of town, the slums, and shine our shoes for us, and mop up our trash, and sit in the last row in the balcony. That's all we ask. And once a week we hang one or two of them. Simple.'

'You don't sound human, and I don't like it.'

'You'll have to get used to it,' he said. He braked the car to a stop before the house and jumped out. 'Find my guns and some rope. We'll do this right.'

'Oh, Willie,' she wailed, and just sat there in the car while he ran up the steps and slammed the front door.

She went along. She didn't want to go along, but he rattled around in the attic, cursing like a crazy man until he found four guns. She saw the brutal metal of them glittering in the black attic, and she couldn't see him at all, he was so dark; she heard only his swearing, and at last his long legs came climbing down from the attic in a shower of dust, and he stacked up bunches of brass shells and blew out the gun chambers and clicked shells into them, his face stern and heavy and folded in upon the gnawing bitterness there. 'Leave us alone,' he kept muttering, his hands flying away from him suddenly, uncontrolled. 'Leave us blame alone, why don't they?'

'Willie, Willie.'

'You too – you too.' And he gave her the same look, and a pressure of his hatred touched her mind.

Outside the window the boys gabbled to each other. 'White as milk, she said. White as milk.'

'White as this old flower, you *see*?'

'White as a stone, like chalk you write with.'

Willie plunged out of the house. 'You children come inside, I'm locking you up. You ain't seeing no white man, you ain't talking about them, you ain't doing nothing. Come on now.'

'But, Daddy –'

He shoved them through the door and went and fetched a bucket of paint and a stencil and from the garage a long thick hairy rope coil into which he fashioned a hangman's knot, very carefully watching the sky while his hands felt their way at their task.

And then they were in the car, leaving bolls of dust behind them down the road. 'Slow up, Willie.'

'This is no slowing-up time,' he said. 'This is a hurrying time, and I'm hurrying.'

All along the road people were looking up in the sky, or climbing in their cars, or riding in cars, and guns were sticking up out of some cars like telescopes sighting all the evils of a world coming to an end.

She looked at the guns. 'You been talking,' she accused her husband.

'That's what I been doing,' he grunted, nodding. He watched the road, fiercely. 'I stopped at every house and I told them what to do, to get their guns, to get paint, to bring rope and be ready. And here we all are, the welcoming committee, to give them the key to the city. Yes, sir!'

She pressed her thin dark hands together to push away the terror growing in her now, and she felt the car bucket and lurch around other cars. She heard the voices yelling, Hey, Willie, look! and hands holding up ropes and guns as they rushed by! and mouths smiling at them in the swift rushing.

'Here we are,' said Willie, and braked the car into dusty halting and silence. He kicked the door open with a big foot and, laden with weapons, stepped out, lugging them across the airport meadow.

'Have you *thought*, Willie?'

'That's all I done for twenty years. I was sixteen when I left Earth, and I was glad to leave,' he said. 'There wasn't anything there for me or you or anybody like us. I've never been sorry I left. We've had peace here, the first time we ever drew a solid breath. Now, come on.'

He pushed through the dark crowd which came to meet him.

'Willie, Willie, what we gonna do?' they said.

'Here's a gun,' he said. 'Here's a gun. Here's another.' He passed them out with savage jabs of his arms. 'Here's a pistol. Here's a shotgun.'

The people were so close together it looked like one dark body with a thousand arms reaching out to take the weapons.

23

'Willie, Willie.'

His wife stood tall and silent by him, her fluted lips pressed shut, and her large eyes wet and tragic. 'Bring the paint,' he said to her. And she lugged a gallon can of yellow paint across the field to where, at that moment, a trolley car was pulling up, with a fresh-painted sign on its front. TO THE WHITE MAN'S LANDING, full of talking people who got off and ran across the meadow, stumbling, looking up. Women with picnic boxes, men with straw hats, in shirt sleeves. The streetcar stood humming and empty. Willie climbed up, set the paint cans down, opened them, stirred the paint, tested a brush, drew forth a stencil, and climbed up on the seat.

'Hey, there!' The conductor came around behind him, his coin changer jangling. 'What you think you're doing? Get down off there!'

'You see what I'm doing. Keep your shirt on.'

And Willie began the stencilling in yellow paint. He dabbed on an F and an O and an R with terrible pride in his work. And when he finished it the conductor squinted up and read the fresh glinting yellow words: FOR WHITES: REAR SECTION. He read it again. FOR WHITES. He blinked. REAR SECTION. The conductor looked at Willie and began to smile.

'Does that suit you?' asked Willie, stepping down.

Said the conductor, 'That suits me just fine, sir.'

Hattie was looking at the sign from outside, and holding her hands over her breasts.

Willie returned to the crowd, which was growing now, taking size from every auto that groaned to a halt, and every new trolley car which squealed around the bend from the nearby town.

Willie climbed up on a packing box. 'Let's have a delegation to paint every streetcar in the next hour. Volunteers?'

Hands leapt up.

'Get going!'

They went.

'Let's have a delegation to fix theatre seats, roped off, the last two rows for whites.'

More hands.

'Go on!'

They ran off.

Willie peered around, bubbled with perspiration, panting with exertion, proud of his energy, his hand on his wife's shoulder who stood under him looking at the ground with her downcast eyes. 'Let's see now,' he declared. 'Oh, yes. We got to pass a law this afternoon; no intermarriages!'

'That's right,' said a lot of people.

'All shoeshine boys quit their jobs today.'

'Quittin' right now!' Some men threw down the rags they carried, in their excitement, all across town.

'Got to pass a minimum wage law, don't we?'

'Sure!'

'Pay them white folks at least ten cents an hour.'

'That's right!'

The mayor of the town hurried up. 'Now look here, Willie Johnson. Get down off that box!'

'Mayor, I can't be made to do nothing like that.'

'You're making a mob, Willie Johnson.'

'That's the idea.'

'The same thing you always hated when you were a kid. You're no better than some of those white men you yell about!'

'This is the other shoe, Mayor, and the other foot,' said Willie, not even looking at the mayor, looking at the faces beneath him, some of them smiling, some of them doubtful, others bewildered, some of them reluctant and drawing away, fearful.

'You'll be sorry,' said the mayor.

'We'll have an election and get a new mayor,' said Willie. And he glanced off at the town where up and down the street signs were being hung, fresh-painted: LIMITED CLIENTELE: *Right to serve customer revokable at any time.* He grinned and slapped his hands. Lord! And streetcars were being halted and sections being painted white in back, to suggest their future inhabitants. And theatres were being invaded and roped off by chuckling men, while their wives stood wondering on the curbs and children were spanked into houses to be hid away from this awful time.

'Are we all ready?' called Willie Johnson, the rope in his hands with the noose tied and neat.

'Ready!' shouted half the crowd. The other half murmured and moved like figures in a nightmare in which they wished no participation.

'Here it comes!' called a small boy.

Like marionette heads on a single string, the heads of the crowd turned upward.

Across the sky, very high and beautiful, a rocket burned on a sweep of orange fire. It circled and came down, causing all to gasp. It landed, setting the meadow afire here and there; the fire burned out, the rocket lay a moment in quiet, and then, as the silent crowd watched, a great door in the side of the vessel whispered out a breath of oxygen, the door slid back and an old man stepped out.

'A white man, a white man, a white man . . .' The words travelled back in the expectant crowd, the children speaking in each other's ears, whispering, butting each other, the words moving in ripples to where the crowd stopped and the street-cars stood in the windy sunlight, the smell of paint coming out their opened windows. The whispering wore itself away and it was gone.

No-one moved.

The white man was tall and straight, but a deep weariness was in his face. He had not shaved this day, and his eyes were as old as the eyes of a man can be and still be alive. His eyes were colourless; almost white and sightless with things he had seen in the passing years. He was as thin as a winter bush. His hands trembled and he had to lean against the portway of the ship as he looked out over the crowd.

He put out a hand and half smiled, but drew his hand back.

No-one moved.

He looked down into their faces, and perhaps he saw but did not see the guns and the ropes, and perhaps he smelled the paint. No-one ever asked him. He began to talk. He started very quietly and slowly, expecting no interruptions, and receiving none, and his voice was very tired and old and pale.

'It doesn't matter who I am,' he said. 'I'd be just a name to you, anyhow. I don't know your names, either. That'll come later.' He paused, closed his eyes for a moment, and then continued:

'Twenty years ago you left Earth. That's a long, long time. It's more like twenty centuries, so much has happened. After you left, the War came.' He nodded slowly. 'Yes, the *big* one. The Third One. It went on for a long time. Until last year. We bombed all of the cities of the world. We destroyed New York and London and Moscow and Paris and Shanghai and Bombay and Alexandria. We ruined it all. And when we finished with the big cities we went to the little cities and atom-bombed and buried them.'

Now he began to name cities and places, and streets. And as he named them, a murmur rose up in his audience.

'We destroyed Natchez . . .'

A murmur.

'And Columbus, Georgia . . .'

Another murmur.

'We burned New Orleans . . .'

A sigh.

'And Atlanta . . .'

Still another.

'And there was nothing left of Greenwater, Alabama.'

Willie Johnson jerked his head and his mouth opened. Hattie saw this gesture, and the recognition coming into his dark eyes.

'Nothing was left,' said the old man in the port, speaking slowly. 'Cotton fields, burned.'

'Oh,' said everyone.

'Cotton mills bombed out –'

'Oh.'

'And the factories, radioactive; everything radioactive. All the roads and the farms and the foods, radioactive. Everything.' He named more names of towns and villages.

'Tampa.'

'That's my town,' someone whispered.

'Fulton.'

'That's mine,' someone else said.

'Memphis.'

'Memphis. Did they burn *Memphis*?' A shocked query.

'Memphis, blown up.'

'*Fourth* Street in Memphis?'

'All of it,' said the old man.

It was stirring them now. After twenty years it was rushing back. The towns and the places, the trees and the brick buildings, the signs and the churches and the familiar stores, all of it was coming to the surface among the gathered people. Each name touched memory, and there was no-one present without a thought of another day. They were all old enough for

27

that, save the children.

'Laredo.'

'I remember Laredo.'

'New York City.'

'I had a store in Harlem.'

'Harlem, bombed out.'

The ominous words. The familiar, remembered places. The struggle to imagine all of those places in ruins.

Willie Johnson murmured the words, 'Greenwater, Alabama. That's where I was born. I remember.'

Gone. All of it gone. The man said so.

The man continued, 'So we destroyed everything and ruined everything, like the fools that we were and the fools that we are. We killed millions. I don't think there were more than five hundred thousand people left in the world, all kinds and types. And out of all the wreckage we salvaged enough metal to build this one rocket, and we came to Mars in it this month to seek your help.'

He hesitated and looked down among the faces to see what could be found there, but he was uncertain.

Hattie Johnson felt her husband's arm tense, saw his fingers grip the rope.

'We've been fools,' said the old man quietly. 'We've brought the Earth and civilization down about our heads. None of the cities are worth saving – they'll be radioactive for a century. Earth is over and done with. Its age is through. You have rockets here which you haven't tried to use to return to Earth in twenty years. Now I've come to ask you to use them. To come to Earth, to pick up the survivors and bring them back to Mars. To help us go on at this time. We've been stupid. Before God we admit our stupidity and our evilness. All the Chinese and the Indians and the Russians and the British and the Americans. We're asking to be taken in. Your Martian soil has lain fallow for numberless centuries; there's room for everyone; it's good soil – I've seen your fields from above. We'll come and work it *for* you. Yes, we'll even do that. We deserve anything you want to do to us, but don't shut us out. We can't force you to act now. If you want I'll get into my ship and go back and that will be all there is to it. We won't bother you again. But we'll come here and we'll work for you and do the things you did for us – clean your houses, cook your meals, shine your shoes, and humble ourselves in the sight of God for the things we have done over the centuries to ourselves, to others, to you.'

He was finished.

There was a silence of silences. A silence you could hold in your hand and a silence that came down like a pressure of a distant storm over the crowd. Their long arms hung like dark pendulums in the sunlight, and their eyes were upon the old man and he did not move now, but waited.

Willie Johnson held the rope in his hands. Those around him watched to see what he might do. His wife Hattie waited, clutching his arm.

She wanted to get at the hate of them all, to pry at it and work at it until she found a little chink, and then pull out a pebble or a stone or a brick and then a part of the wall, and, once started, the whole edifice might roar down and be done away with. It was teetering now. But which was the keystone, and how to get at it? How to touch them and get a thing started in all of them to make a ruin of their hate?

She looked at Willie there in the strong silence and the only thing she knew about the situation was him and his life and what had happened to him, and suddenly he was the keystone; suddenly she knew that if he could be pried loose, then the thing in all of them might be loosened and torn away.

'Mister –' She stepped forward. She didn't even know the first words to say. The crowd stared at her back; she felt them staring. 'Mister –'

The man turned to her with a tired smile.

'Mister,' she said, 'do you know Knockwood Hill in Greenwater, Alabama?'

The old man spoke over his shoulder to someone within the ship. A moment later a photographic map was handed out and the man held it, waiting.

'You know the big oak on top of that hill, mister?'

The big oak. The place where Willie's father was shot and hung and found swinging in the morning wind.

'Yes.'

'Is that still there?' asked Hattie.

'It's gone,' said the old man. 'Blown up. The hill's all gone, and the oak tree too. You see?' He touched the photograph.

'Let me see that,' said Willie, jerking forward and looking at

29

the map.

Hattie blinked at the white man, heart pounding.

'Tell me about Greenwater,' she said quickly.

'What do you want to know?'

'About Dr Phillips. Is he still alive?'

A moment in which the information was found in a clicking machine within the rocket . . .

'Killed in the war.'

'And his son?'

'Dead.'

'What about their house?'

'Burned. Like all the other houses.'

'What about that other big tree on Knockwood Hill?'

'All the trees went – burned.'

'*That* tree went, you're sure?' said Willie.

'Yes.'

Willie's blood loosened somewhat.

'And what about that Mr Burton's house and Mr Burton?'

'No houses at all left, no people.'

'You know Mrs Johnson's washing shack, my mother's place?'

The place where she was shot.

'That's gone too. Everything's gone. Here are the pictures, you can see for yourself.'

The pictures were there to be held and looked at and thought about. The rocket was full of pictures and answers to questions. Any town, any building, any place.

Willie stood with the rope in his hands.

He was remembering Earth, the green Earth and the green town where he was born and raised, and he was thinking now of that town, gone to pieces, to ruin, blown up and scattered, all of the landmarks with it, all of the supposed or certain evil scattered with it, all of the hard men gone, the stables, the ironsmiths, the curio shops, the soda founts, the gin mills, the river bridges, the lynching trees, the buckshot-covered hills, the roads, the cows, the mimosas, and his own house as well as those big-pillared houses down near the long river, those white mortuaries where the women as delicate as moths fluttered in the autumn light, distant, far away. Those houses where the cold men rocked, with glasses of drink in their hands, guns leaned against the porch newels, sniffing the autumn airs and considering death. Gone, all gone; gone and never coming back. Now, for certain, all of that civilization ripped into confetti and strewn at their feet. Nothing, nothing of it left to hate – not an empty brass gun shell, or a twisted hemp, or a tree, or even a hill of it to hate. Nothing but some alien people in a rocket, people who might shine his shoes and ride in the back of trolleys or sit far up in midnight theatres . . .

'You won't have to do that,' said Willie Johnson.

His wife glanced at his big hands.

His fingers were opening.

The rope, released, fell and coiled upon itself along the ground.

They ran through the streets of their town and tore down the new signs so quickly made, and painted out the fresh yellow signs on streetcars, and they cut down the ropes in the theatre balconies, and unloaded their guns and stacked their ropes away.

'A new start for everyone,' said Hattie, on the way home in their car.

'Yes,' said Willie at last. 'The Lord's let us come through, a few here and a few there. And what happens next is up to all of us. The time for being fools is over. We got to be something else except fools. I knew that when he talked. I knew then that now the white man's as lonely as we've always been. He's got no home now, just like we didn't have one for so long. Now everything's even. We can start all over again, on the same level.'

He stopped the car and sat in it, not moving, while Hattie went to let the children out. They ran down to see their father. 'You see the white man? You see him?' they cried.

'Yes, sir,' said Willie, sitting behind the wheel, rubbing his face with his slow fingers. 'Seems like for the first time today I really seen the white man – I really seen him clear.'

The Destructors

GRAHAM GREENE

1

It was on the eve of August Bank Holiday that the latest recruit became the leader of the Wormsley Common Gang. No one was surprised except Mike, but Mike at the age of nine was surprised by everything. 'If you don't shut your mouth,' somebody once said to him, 'you'll get a frog down it.' After that Mike kept his teeth tightly clamped except when the surprise was too great.

The new recruit had been with the gang since the beginning of the summer holidays, and there were possibilities about his brooding silence that all recognized. He never wasted a word even to tell his name until that was required of him by the rules. When he said 'Trevor' it was a statement of fact, not as it would have been with the others a statement of shame or defiance. Nor did anyone laugh except Mike, who finding himself without support and meeting the dark gaze of the newcomer opened his mouth and was quiet again. There was every reason why T., as he was afterwards referred to, should have been an object of mockery – there was his name (and they substituted the initial because otherwise they had no excuse not to laugh at it), the fact that his father, a former architect and present clerk, had 'come down in the world' and that his mother considered herself better than the neighbours. What but an odd quality of danger, of the unpredictable, established him in the gang without any ignoble ceremony of initiation?

The gang met every morning in an impromptu car-park, the site of the last bomb of the first blitz. The leader, who was known as Blackie, claimed to have heard it fall, and no one was precise enough in his dates to point out that he would have been one year old and fast asleep on the down platform of Wormsley Common Underground Station. On one side of the car-park leant the first occupied house, No 3, of the shattered Northwood Terrace – literally leant, for it had suffered from the blast of the bomb and the side walls were supported on

32

wooden struts. A smaller bomb and incendiaries had fallen beyond, so that the house stuck up like a jagged tooth and carried on the further wall relics of its neighbour, a dado, the remains of a fireplace. T., whose words were almost confined to voting 'Yes' or 'No' to the plan of operations proposed each day by Blackie, once startled the whole gang by saying broodingly, 'Wren built that house, father says.'

'Who's Wren?'

'The man who built St Paul's.'

'Who cares?' Blackie said. 'It's only Old Misery's.'

Old Misery – whose real name was Thomas – had once been a builder and decorator. He lived alone in the crippled house, doing for himself: once a week you could see him coming back across the common with bread and vegetables, and once as the boys played in the car-park he put his head over the smashed wall of his garden and looked at them.

'Been to the lav,' one of the boys said, for it was common knowledge that since the bombs fell something had gone wrong with the pipes of the house and Old Misery was too mean to spend money on the property. He could do the redecorating himself at cost price, but he had never learnt plumbing. The lav was a wooden shed at the bottom of the narrow garden with a star-shaped hole in the door: it had escaped the blast which had smashed the house next door and sucked out the window-frames of No 3.

The next time the gang became aware of Mr Thomas was more surprising. Blackie, Mike and a thin yellow boy, who for some reason was called by his surname Summers, met him on the common coming back from the market. Mr Thomas stopped them. He said glumly, 'You belong to the lot that play in the car-park?'

Mike was about to answer when Blackie stopped him. As the leader he had responsibilities. 'Suppose we are?' he said ambiguously.

'I got some chocolates,' Mr Thomas said. 'Don't like 'em myself. Here you are. Not enough to go round, I don't suppose. There never is,' he added with sombre conviction. He handed over three packets of Smarties.

The gang was puzzled and perturbed by this action and tried to explain it away. 'Bet someone dropped them and he picked 'em up,' somebody suggested.

'Pinched 'em and then got in a bleeding funk,' another thought aloud.

'It's a bribe,' Summers said. 'He wants us to stop bouncing balls on his wall.'

'We'll show him we don't take bribes,' Blackie said, and they sacrificed the whole morning to the game of bouncing that only Mike was young enough to enjoy. There was no sign from Mr Thomas.

Next day T. astonished them all. He was late at the rendezvous, and the voting for that day's exploit took place without him. At Blackie's suggestion the gang was to disperse in pairs, take buses at random and see how many free rides could be snatched from unwary conductors (the operation was to be carried out in pairs to avoid cheating). They were drawing lots for their companions when T. arrived.

'Where you been, T.?' Blackie asked. 'You can't vote now. You know the rules.'

'I've been *there*,' T. said. He looked at the ground, as though he had thoughts to hide.

'Where?'

'At Old Misery's.' Mike's mouth opened and then hurriedly closed again with a click. He had remembered the frog.

'At Old Misery's?' Blackie said. There was nothing in the rules against it, but he had a sensation that T. was treading on dangerous ground. He asked hopefully, 'Did you break in?'

'No. I rang the bell.'

'And what did you say?'

'I said I wanted to see his house.'

'What did he do?'

'He showed it me.'

'Pinch anything?'

'No.'

'What did you do it for then?'

The gang had gathered round; it was as though an impromptu court were about to form and try some case of deviation. T. said, 'It's a beautiful house,' and still watching the ground, meeting no one's eyes, he licked his lips first one way, then the other.

'What do you mean, a beautiful house?' Blackie asked with scorn.

'It's got a staircase two hundred years old like a corkscrew.

35

Nothing holds it up.'

'What do you mean, nothing holds it up. Does it float?'

'It's to do with opposite forces, Old Misery said.'

'What else?'

'There's panelling.'

'Like in the Blue Boar?'

'Two hundred years old.'

'Is Old Misery two hundred years old?'

Mike laughed suddenly and then was quiet again. The meeting was in a serious mood. For the first time since T. had strolled into the car-park on the first day of the holidays his position was in danger. It only needed a single use of his real name and the gang would be at his heels.

'What did you do it for?' Blackie asked. He was just, he had no jealousy, he was anxious to retain T. in the gang if he could. It was the word 'beautiful' that worried him – that belonged to a class world that you could still see parodied at the Wormsley Common Empire by a man wearing a top hat and a monocle, with a haw-haw accent. He was tempted to say, 'My dear Trevor, old chap,' and unleash his hell hounds. 'If you'd broken in,' he said sadly – that indeed would have been an exploit worthy of the gang.

'This was better,' T. said. 'I found out things.' He continued to stare at his feet, not meeting anybody's eye, as though he were absorbed in some dream he was unwilling – or ashamed – to share.

'What things?'

'Old Misery's going to be away all tomorrow and Bank Holiday.'

Blackie said with relief, 'You mean we could break in?'

'And pinch things?' somebody asked.

Blackie said, 'Nobody's going to pinch things. Breaking in – that's good enough, isn't it? We don't want any court stuff.'

'I don't want to pinch anything,' T. said. 'I've got a better idea.'

'What is it?'

T. raised eyes, as grey and disturbed as the drab August day. 'We'll pull it down,' he said. 'We'll destroy it.'

Blackie gave a single hoot of laughter and then, like Mike, fell quiet, daunted by the serious implacable gaze. 'What'd the police be doing all the time?' he said.

36

'They'd never know. We'd do it from inside. I've found a way in.' He said with a sort of intensity, 'We'd be like worms, don't you see, in an apple. When we came out again there'd be nothing there, no staircase, no panels, nothing but just walls, and then we'd make the walls fall down – somehow.'

'We'd go to jug,' Blackie said.

'Who's to prove? and anyway we wouldn't have pinched anything.' He added without the smallest flicker of glee, 'There wouldn't be anything to pinch after we'd finished.'

'I've never heard of going to prison for breaking things,' Summers said.

'There wouldn't be time,' Blackie said. 'I've seen house-breakers at work.'

'There are twelve of us,' T. said. 'We'd organize.'

'None of us know how . . .'

'I know,' T. said. He looked at Blackie. 'Have you got a better plan?'

'Today,' Mike said tactlessly, 'we're pinching free rides . . .'

'Free rides,' T. said. 'Kid stuff. You can stand down, Blackie, if you'd rather . . .'

'The gang's got to vote.'

'Put it up then.'

Blackie said uneasily, 'It's proposed that tomorrow and Monday we destroy Old Misery's house.'

'Here, here,' said a fat boy called Joe.

'Who's in favour?'

T. said, 'It's carried.'

'How do we start?' Summers asked.

'He'll tell you,' Blackie said. It was the end of his leadership. He went away to the back of the car-park and began to kick a stone, dribbling it this way and that. There was only one old Morris in the park, for few cars were left there except lorries: without an attendant there was no safety. He took a flying kick at the car and scraped a little paint off the rear mudguard. Beyond, paying no more attention to him than to a stranger, the gang had gathered round T.; Blackie was dimly aware of the fickleness of favour. He thought of going home, of never returning, of letting them all discover the hollowness of T.'s leadership, but suppose after all what T. proposed was possible – nothing like it had ever been done before. The fame of the Wormsley Common car-park gang would surely reach around

37

London. There would be headlines in the papers. Even the grown-up gangs who ran the betting at the all-in wrestling and the barrow-boys would hear with respect of how Old Misery's house had been destroyed. Driven by the pure, simple and altruistic ambition of fame for the gang, Blackie came back to where T. stood in the shadow of Old Misery's wall.

T. was giving his orders with decision: it was as though this plan had been with him all his life, pondered through the seasons, now in his fifteenth year crystallized with the pain of puberty. 'You,' he said to Mike, 'bring some big nails, the biggest you can find, and a hammer. Anybody who can, better bring a hammer and a screwdriver. We'll need plenty of them. Chisels too. We can't have too many chisels. Can anybody bring a saw?'

'I can,' Mike said.

'Not a child's saw,' T. said. 'A real saw.'

Blackie realized he had raised his hand like any ordinary member of the gang.

'Right, you bring one, Blackie. But now there's a difficulty. We want a hacksaw.'

'What's a hacksaw?' someone asked.

'You can get 'em at Woolworth's,' Summers said.

The fat boy called Joe said gloomily, 'I knew it would end in a collection.'

'I'll get one myself,' T. said. 'I don't want your money. But I can't buy a sledge-hammer.'

Blackie said, 'They are working on No 15. I know where they'll leave their stuff for Bank Holiday.'

'Then that's all,' T. said. 'We meet here at nine sharp.'

'I've got to go to church,' Mike said.

'Come over the wall and whistle. We'll let you in.'

2

On Sunday morning all were punctual except Blackie, even Mike. Mike had a stroke of luck. His mother felt ill, his father was tired after Saturday night, and he was told to go to church alone with many warnings of what would happen if he strayed. Blackie had difficulty in smuggling out the saw, and then in finding the sledge-hammer at the back of No 15. He approached the house from a lane at the rear of the garden, for fear of the policeman's beat along the main road. The tired evergreens kept off a stormy sun; another wet Bank Holiday was being prepared over the Atlantic, beginning in swirls of dust under the trees. Blackie climbed the wall into Misery's garden.

There was no sign of anybody anywhere. The lav stood like a tomb in a neglected graveyard. The curtains were drawn. The house slept. Blackie lumbered nearer with the saw and the sledge-hammer. Perhaps after all nobody had turned up: the plan had been a wild invention: they had woken wiser. But when he came close to the back door he could hear a confusion of sound hardly louder than a hive in swarm: a clickety-clack, a bang bang, a scraping, a creaking, a sudden painful crack. He thought: it's true, and whistled.

They opened the back door to him and he came in. He had at once the impression of organization, very different from the old happy-go-lucky ways under his leadership. For a while he wandered up and down stairs looking for T. Nobody addressed him: he had a sense of great urgency, and already he could begin to see the plan. The interior of the house was being carefully demolished without touching the walls. Summers with hammer and chisel was ripping out the skirting-boards in the ground floor dining-room: he had already smashed the panels of the door. In the same room Joe was heaving up the parquet blocks, exposing the soft wood floorboards over the cellar. Coils of wire came out of the damaged skirting and Mike sat happily on the floor clipping the wires.

On the curved stairs two of the gang were working hard with an inadequate child's saw on the banisters – when they saw Blackie's big saw they signalled for it wordlessly. When he next saw them a quarter of the banisters had been dropped into the hall. He found T. at last in the bathroom – he sat moodily in the least cared-for room in the house, listening to the sounds coming up from below.

'You've really done it,' Blackie said with awe. 'What's going to happen?'

'We've only just begun,' T. said. He looked at the sledge-hammer and gave his instructions. 'You stay here and break the bath and the wash-basin. Don't bother about the pipes. They come later.'

Mike appeared at the door. 'I've finished the wires, T.,' he said.

'Good. You've just got to go wandering round now. The kitchen's in the basement. Smash all the china and glass and bottles you can lay hold of. Don't turn on the taps – we don't want a flood – yet. Then go into all the rooms and turn out the drawers. If they are locked get one of the others to break them open. Tear up any papers you find and smash all the ornaments. Better take a carving knife with you from the kitchen. The bedroom's opposite here. Open the pillows and tear up the sheets. That's enough for the moment. And you, Blackie, when you've finished in here crack the plaster in the passage up with your sledge-hammer.'

'What are you going to do?' Blackie asked.

'I'm looking for something special,' T. said.

It was nearly lunch-time before Blackie had finished and went in search of T. Chaos had advanced. The kitchen was a shambles of broken glass and china. The dining-room was stripped of parquet, the skirting was up, the door had been taken off its hinges, and the destroyers had moved up a floor. Streaks of light came in through the closed shutters where they worked with the seriousness of creators – and destruction after all is a form of creation. A kind of imagination had seen this house as it had now become.

Mike said, 'I've got to go home for dinner.'

'Who else?' T. asked, but all the others on one excuse or another had brought provisions with them.

They squatted in the ruins of the room and swapped unwanted sandwiches. Half an hour for lunch and they were at work again. By the time Mike returned they were on the top floor, and by six the superficial damage was completed. The doors were all off, all the skirtings raised, the furniture pillaged and ripped and smashed – no one could have slept in the house except on a bed of broken plaster. T. gave his orders – eight o'clock next morning, and to escape notice they climbed singly over the garden wall, into the car-park. Only Blackie and T. were left: the light had nearly gone, and when they touched a switch, nothing worked – Mike had done his job thoroughly.

'Did you find anything special?' Blackie asked.

T. nodded. 'Come over here,' he said, 'and look.' Out of both pockets he drew bundles of pound notes. 'Old Misery's savings,' he said. 'Mike ripped out the mattress, but he missed them.'

40

'What are you going to do? Share them?'

'We aren't thieves,' T. said. 'Nobody's going to steal anything from this house. I kept these for you and me – a celebration.' He knelt down on the floor and counted them out – there were seventy in all. 'We'll burn them,' he said, 'one by one,' and taking it in turns they held a note upwards and lit the top corner, so that the flame burnt slowly towards their fingers. The grey ash floated above them and fell on their heads like age. 'I'd like to see Old Misery's face when we are through,' T. said.

'You hate him a lot?' Blackie asked.

'Of course I don't hate him,' T. said. 'There'd be no fun if I hated him.' The last burning note illuminated his brooding face. 'All this hate and love,' he said, 'it's soft, it's hooey. There's only things, Blackie,' and he looked round the room crowded with the unfamiliar shadows of half things, broken things, former things. 'I'll race you home, Blackie,' he said.

3

Next morning the serious destruction started. Two were missing – Mike and another boy whose parents were off to Southend and Brighton in spite of the slow warm drops that had begun to fall and the rumble of thunder in the estuary like the first guns of the old blitz. 'We've got to hurry,' T. said.

Summers was restive. 'Haven't we done enough?' he asked. 'I've been given a bob for slot machines. This is like work.'

'We've hardly started,' T. said. 'Why, there's all the floors left, and the stairs. We haven't taken out a single window. You voted like the others. We are going to *destroy* this house. There won't be anything left when we've finished.'

They began again on the first floor picking up the top floor-boards next to the outer wall, leaving the joists exposed. Then they sawed through the joists and retreated into the hall, as what was left of the floor heeled and sank. They had learnt with practice, and the second floor collapsed more easily. By the evening an odd exhilaration seized them as they looked down the great hollow of the house. They ran risks and made mistakes: when they thought of the windows it was too late to reach them. 'Cor,' Joe said, and dropped a penny down into the dry rubble-filled well. It cracked and span amongst the broken glass.

'Why did we start this?' Summers asked with astonishm_nt; T. was already on the ground, digging at the rubble, clearing a space along the outer wall. 'Turn on the taps,' he said. 'It's too dark for anyone to see now, and in the morning it won't matter.' The water overtook them on the stairs and fell through the floorless rooms.

It was then they heard Mike's whistle at the back. 'Something's wrong,' Blackie said. They could hear his urgent breathing as they unlocked the door.

'The bogies?' Summers asked.

'Old Misery,' Mike said. 'He's on his way,' he said with pride.

'But why?' T. said, 'He told me . . .' He protested with the fury of the child he had never been, 'It isn't fair.'

'He was down at Southend,' Mike said, 'and he was on the train coming back. Said it was too cold and wet.' He paused and gazed at the water. 'My, you've had a storm here. Is the roof leaking?'

'How long will he be?'

'Five minutes. I gave Ma the slip and ran.'

'We better clear,' Summers said. 'We've done enough, anyway.'

'Oh no, we haven't. Anybody could do this –' 'this' was the shattered hollowed house with nothing left but the walls. Yet walls could be preserved. Façades were valuable. They could build inside again more beautifully than before. This could again be a home. He said angrily, 'We've got to finish. Don't move. Let me think.'

'There's no time,' a boy said.

'There's got to be a way,' T. said. 'We couldn't have got this far . . .'

'We've done a lot,' Blackie said.

'No. No, we haven't. Somebody watch the front.'

'We can't do any more.'

'He may come in at the back.'

'Watch the back too.' T. began to plead. 'Just give me a minute and I'll fix it. I swear I'll fix it.' But his authority had gone with his ambiguity. He was only one of the gang. 'Please,' he said.

'Please,' Summers mimicked him, and then suddenly struck home with the fatal name. 'Run along home, Trevor.'

42

T. stood with his back to the rubble like a boxer knocked groggy against the ropes. He had no words as his dreams shook and slid. Then Blackie acted before the gang had time to laugh, pushing Summers backward. 'I'll watch the front, T.,' he said, and cautiously he opened the shutters of the hall. The grey wet common stretched ahead, and the lamps gleamed in the puddles. 'Someone's coming, T. No, it's not him. What's your plan, T.?'

'Tell Mike to go out to the lav and hide close beside it. When he hears me whistle he's got to count ten and start to shout.'

'Shout what?'

'Oh, "Help", anything.'

'You hear, Mike,' Blackie said. He was the leader again. He took a quick look between the shutters. 'He's coming, T.'

'Quick, Mike. The lav. Stay here, Blackie, all of you, till I yell.'

'Where are you going, T.?'

'Don't worry. I'll see to this. I said I would, didn't I?'

Old Misery came limping off the common. He had mud on his shoes and he stopped to scrape them on the pavement's edge. He didn't want to soil his house, which stood jagged and dark between the bomb-sites, saved so narrowly, as he believed, from destruction. Even the fan-light had been left unbroken by the bomb's blast. Somewhere somebody whistled. Old Misery looked sharply round. He didn't trust whistles. A child was shouting: it seemed to come from his own garden. Then a boy ran into the road from the car-park. 'Mr Thomas,' he called, 'Mr Thomas.'

'What is it?'

'I'm terribly sorry, Mr Thomas. One of us got taken short, and we thought you wouldn't mind, and now he can't get out.'

'What do you mean, boy?'

'He's got stuck in your lav.'

'He'd no business . . . Haven't I seen you before?'

'You showed me your house.'

'So I did. So I did. That doesn't give you the right to . . .'

'Do hurry, Mr Thomas. He'll suffocate.'

'Nonsense. He can't suffocate. Wait till I put my bag in.'

'I'll carry your bag.'

'Oh no, you don't. I carry my own.'

'This way, Mr Thomas.'

'I can't get in the garden that way. I've got to go through the house.'

'But you *can* get in the garden this way, Mr Thomas. We often do.'

'You often do?' He followed the boy with a scandalized fascination. 'When? What right . . .?'

'Do you see . . .? the wall's low.'

'I'm not going to climb walls into my own garden. It's absurd.'

'This is how we do it. One foot here, one foot there, and over.' The boy's face peered down, an arm shot out, and Mr Thomas found his bag taken and deposited on the other side of the wall.

'Give me back my bag,' Mr Thomas said. From the loo a boy yelled and yelled. 'I'll call the police.'

'Your bag's all right, Mr Thomas. Look. One foot there. On your right. Now just above. To your left.' Mr Thomas climbed over his own garden wall. 'Here's your bag, Mr Thomas.'

'I'll have the wall built up,' Mr Thomas said, 'I'll not have you boys coming over here, using my loo.' He stumbled on the path, but the boy caught his elbow and supported him. 'Thank you, thank you, my boy,' he murmured automatically. Somebody shouted again through the dark. 'I'm coming, I'm coming,' Mr Thomas called. He said to the boy beside him, 'I'm not unreasonable. Been a boy myself. As long as things are done regular, I don't mind you playing round the place Saturday mornings. Sometimes I like company. Only it's got to be regular. One of you asks leave and I say Yes. Sometimes I'll say No. Won't feel like it. And you come in at the front door and out at the back. No garden walls.'

'Do get him out, Mr Thomas.'

'He won't come to any harm in my loo,' Mr Thomas said, stumbling slowly down the garden. 'Oh, my rheumatics,' he said. 'Always get 'em on Bank Holiday. I've got to be careful. There's loose stones here. Give me your hand. Do you know what my horoscope said yesterday? "Abstain from any dealings in first half of week. Danger of serious crash." That might be on this path,' Mr Thomas said. 'They speak in parables and double meanings.' He paused at the door of the loo. 'What's the matter in there?' he called. There was no reply.

'Perhaps he's fainted,' the boy said.

'Not in my loo. Here, you, come out,' Mr Thomas said, and giving a great jerk at the door he nearly fell on his back when it swung easily open. A hand first supported him and then pushed him hard. His head hit the opposite wall and he sat heavily down. His bag hit his feet. A hand whipped the key out of the lock and the door slammed. 'Let me out,' he called, and heard the key turn in the lock. 'A serious crash,' he thought, and felt dithery and confused and old.

A voice spoke to him softly through the star-shaped hole in the door. 'Don't worry, Mr Thomas,' it said, 'we won't hurt you, not if you stay quiet.'

Mr Thomas put his head between his hands and pondered. He had noticed that there was only one lorry in the car-park, and he felt certain that the driver would not come for it before the morning. Nobody could hear him from the road in front, and the lane at the back was seldom used. Anyone who passed there would be hurrying home and would not pause for what they would certainly take to be drunken cries. And if he did call 'Help', who, on a lonely Bank Holiday evening, would have the courage to investigate? Mr Thomas sat on the loo and pondered with the wisdom of age.

After a while it seemed to him that there were sounds in the silence – they were faint and came from the direction of his house. He stood up and peered through the ventilation-hole – between the cracks in one of the shutters he saw a light, not the light of a lamp, but the wavering light that a candle might give. Then he thought he heard the sound of hammering and scraping and chipping. He thought of burglars – perhaps they had employed the boy as a scout, but why should burglars engage in what sounded more and more like a stealthy form of carpentry? Mr Thomas let out an experimental yell, but nobody answered. The noise could not even have reached his enemies.

4

Mike had gone home to bed, but the rest stayed. The question of leadership no longer concerned the gang. With nails, chisels, screwdrivers, anything that was sharp and penetrating, they moved around the inner walls worrying at the mortar between the bricks. They started too high, and it was Blackie who hit on the damp course and realized the work could be halved if they weakened the joints immediately above. It was a long, tiring, unamusing job, but at last it was finished. The gutted house stood there balanced on a few inches of mortar between the damp course and the bricks.

There remained the most dangerous task of all, out in the open at the edge of the bomb-site. Summers was sent to watch the road for passers-by, and Mr Thomas, sitting on the loo, heard clearly now the sound of sawing. It no longer came from the house, and that a little reassured him. He felt less concerned. Perhaps the other noises too had no significance.

A voice spoke to him through the hole. 'Mr Thomas.'

'Let me out,' Mr Thomas said sternly.

'Here's a blanket,' the voice said, and a long grey sausage was worked through the hole and fell in swathes over Mr Thomas's head.

'There's nothing personal,' the voice said. 'We want you to be comfortable tonight.'

'Tonight,' Mr Thomas repeated incredulously.

'Catch,' the voice said. 'Penny buns – we've buttered them, and sausage-rolls. We don't want you to starve, Mr Thomas.'

Mr Thomas pleaded desperately. 'A joke's a joke, boy. Let me out and I won't say a thing. I've got rheumatics. I got to sleep comfortable.'

'You wouldn't be comfortable, not in your house, you wouldn't. Not now.'

'What do you mean, boy?' But the footsteps receded. There was only the silence of night: no sound of sawing. Mr Thomas tried one more yell, but he was daunted and rebuked by the silence – a long way off an owl hooted and made away again on its muffled flight through the soundless world.

At seven next morning the driver came to fetch his lorry. He climbed into the seat and tried to start the engine. He was vaguely aware of a voice shouting, but it didn't concern him. At last the engine responded and he backed the lorry until it touched the great wooden shore that supported Mr Thomas's house. That way he could drive right out and down the street without reversing. The lorry moved forward, was momentarily checked as though something were pulling it from behind, and then went on to the sound of a long rumbling crash. The driver was astonished to see bricks bouncing ahead of him, while stones hit the roof of his cab. He put on his brakes. When he climbed out the whole landscape had suddenly altered. There was no house beside the car-park, only a hill of rubble. He went round and examined the back of his lorry for damage, and found a rope tied there that was still twisted at the other end round part of a wooden strut.

The driver again became aware of somebody shouting. It came from the wooden erection which was the nearest thing to a house in that desolation of broken brick. The driver climbed the smashed wall and unlocked the door. Mr Thomas came out of the loo. He was wearing a grey blanket to which flakes of pastry adhered. He gave a sobbing cry. 'My house,' he said. 'Where's my house?'

'Search me,' the driver said. His eye lit on the remains of a bath and what had once been a dresser and he began to laugh. There wasn't anything left anywhere.

'How dare you laugh,' Mr Thomas said. 'It was my house. My house.'

'I'm sorry,' the driver said, making heroic efforts, but when he remembered the sudden check of his lorry, the crash of bricks falling, he became convulsed again. One moment the house had stood there with such dignity between the bomb-sites like a man in a top hat, and then, bang, crash, there wasn't anything left – not anything. He said, 'I'm sorry. I can't help it, Mr Thomas. There's nothing personal, but you got to admit it's funny.'

Lamb to the Slaughter

ROALD DAHL

The room was warm and clean, the curtains drawn, the two table lamps alight – hers and the one by the empty chair opposite. On the sideboard behind her, two tall glasses, soda water, whisky. Fresh ice cubes in the Thermos bucket.

Mary Maloney was waiting for her husband to come home from work.

Now and again she would glance up at the clock, but without anxiety, merely to please herself with the thought that each minute gone by made it nearer the time when he would come. There was a slow smiling air about her, and about everything she did. The drop of the head as she bent over her sewing was curiously tranquil. Her skin – for this was her sixth month with child – had acquired a wonderful translucent quality, the mouth was soft, and the eyes, with their new placid look, seemed larger, darker than before.

When the clock said ten minutes to five, she began to listen, and a few moments later, punctually as always, she heard the tyres on the gravel outside, and the car door slamming, the footsteps passing the window, the key turning in the lock. She laid aside her sewing, stood up, and went forward to kiss him as he came in.

'Hullo, darling,' she said.

'Hullo,' he answered.

She took his coat and hung it in the closet. Then she walked over and made the drinks, a strongish one for him, a weak one for herself; and soon she was back again in her chair with the sewing, and he in the other, opposite, holding the tall glass with both his hands, rocking it so the ice cubes tinkled against the side.

For her, this was always a blissful time of day. She knew he didn't want to speak much until the first drink was finished, and she, on her side, was content to sit quietly, enjoying his company after the long hours alone in the house. She loved to luxuriate in the presence of this man, and to feel – almost as a sunbather feels the sun – that warm male glow that came out of him to her when they were alone together. She loved him for the way he sat loosely in a chair, for the way he came in a door, or moved slowly across the room with long strides. She loved the intent, far look in his eyes when they rested on her, the funny shape of the mouth, and especially the way he remained silent about his tiredness, sitting still with himself until the whisky had taken some of it away.

'Tired, darling?'

'Yes,' he said. 'I'm tired.' And as he spoke, he did an unusual thing. He lifted his glass and drained it in one swallow although there was still half of it, at least half of it, left. She wasn't really watching him but she knew what he had done because she heard the ice cubes falling back against the bottom of the empty glass when he lowered his arm. He paused a moment, leaning forward in the chair, then he got up and went slowly over to fetch himself another.

'I'll get it!' she cried, jumping up.

'Sit down,' he said.

When he came back, she noticed that the new drink was dark amber with the quantity of whisky in it.

'Darling, shall I get your slippers?'

'No.'

She watched him as he began to sip the dark yellow drink, and she could see little oily swirls in the liquid because it was so strong.

'I think it's a shame,' she said, 'that when a policeman gets to be as senior as you, they keep him walking about on his feet all day long.'

He didn't answer, so she bent her head again and went on with her sewing; but each time he lifted the drink to his lips, she heard the ice cubes clinking against the side of the glass.

'Darling,' she said. 'Would you like me to get you some cheese? I haven't made any supper because it's Thursday.'

'No,' he said.

'If you're too tired to eat out,' she went on, 'it's still not too late. There's plenty of meat and stuff in the freezer, and you can have it right here and not even move out of the chair.'

Her eyes waited on him for an answer, a smile, a little nod, but he made no sign.

'Anyway,' she went on, 'I'll get you some cheese and crackers

49

first.'

'I don't want it,' he said.

She moved uneasily in her chair, the large eyes still watching his face. 'But you *must* have supper. I can easily do it here. I'd like to do it. We can have lamb chops. Or pork. Anything you want. Everything's in the freezer.'

'Forget it,' he said.

'But, darling, you *must* eat! I'll fix it anyway, and then you can have it or not, as you like.'

She stood up and placed her sewing on the table by the lamp.

'Sit down,' he said. 'Just for a minute, sit down.'

It wasn't till then that she began to get frightened.

'Go on,' he said. 'Sit down.'

She lowered herself back slowly into the chair, watching him all the time with those large, bewildered eyes. He had finished the second drink and was staring into the glass, frowning.

'Listen,' he said, 'I've got something to tell you.'

'What is it, darling? What's the matter?'

He had become absolutely motionless, and he kept his head down so that the light from the lamp beside him fell across the upper part of his face, leaving the chin and mouth in shadow. She noticed there was a little muscle moving near the corner of his left eye.

'This is going to be a bit of a shock to you, I'm afraid,' he said. 'But I've thought about it a good deal and I've decided the only thing to do is tell you right away. I hope you won't blame me too much.'

And he told her. It didn't take long, four or five minutes at most, and she sat very still through it all, watching him with a kind of dazed horror as he went further and further away from her with each word.

'So there it is,' he added. 'And I know it's kind of a bad time to be telling you, but there simply wasn't any other way. Of course I'll give you money and see you're looked after. But there needn't really be any fuss. I hope not anyway. It wouldn't be very good for my job.'

Her first instinct was not to believe any of it, to reject it all. It occurred to her that perhaps he hadn't even spoken, that she herself had imagined the whole thing. Maybe, if she went about her business and acted as though she hadn't been listening, then later, when she sort of woke up again, she might find none of it had ever happened.

'I'll get the supper,' she managed to whisper, and this time he didn't stop her.

When she walked across the room she couldn't feel her feet touching the floor. She couldn't feel anything at all – except a slight nausea and a desire to vomit. Everything was automatic now – down the stairs to the cellar, the light switch, the deep freeze, the hand inside the cabinet taking hold of the first object it met. She lifted it out, and looked at it. It was wrapped in paper, so she took off the paper and looked at it again.

A leg of lamb.

All right then, they would have lamb for supper. She carried it upstairs, holding the thin bone-end of it with both her hands, and as she went through the living-room, she saw him standing over by the window with his back to her, and she stopped.

'For God's sake,' he said, hearing her, but not turning round, 'Don't make supper for me. I'm going out.'

At that point, Mary Maloney simply walked up behind him and without any pause she swung the big frozen leg of lamb high in the air and brought it down as hard as she could on the back of his head.

She might just as well have hit him with a steel club.

She stepped back a pace, waiting, and the funny thing was that he remained standing there for at least four or five seconds, gently swaying. Then he crashed to the carpet.

The violence of the crash, the noise, the small table over-turning, helped bring her out of the shock. She came out slowly, feeling cold and surprised, and she stood for a while blinking at the body, still holding the ridiculous piece of meat tight with both hands.

All right, she told herself. So I've killed him.

It was extraordinary, now, how clear her mind became all of a sudden. She began thinking very fast. As the wife of a detective, she knew quite well what the penalty would be. That was fine. It made no difference to her. In fact, it would be a relief. On the other hand, what about the child? What were the laws about murderers with unborn children? Did they kill them both – mother and child? Or did they wait until the tenth month? What did they do?

51

52

Mary Maloney didn't know. And she certainly wasn't prepared to take a chance.

She carried the meat into the kitchen, placed it in a pan, turned the oven on high, and shoved it inside. Then she washed her hands and ran upstairs to the bedroom. She sat down before the mirror, tidied her face, touched up her lips and face. She tried a smile. It came out rather peculiar. She tried again.

'Hullo Sam,' she said brightly, aloud.

The voice sounded peculiar too.

'I want some potatoes please, Sam. Yes, and I think a can of peas.'

That was better. Both the smile and the voice were coming out better now. She rehearsed it several times more. Then she ran downstairs, took her coat, went out the back door, down the garden, into the street.

It wasn't six o'clock yet and the lights were still on in the grocery shop.

'Hullo Sam,' she said brightly, smiling at the man behind the counter.

'Why, good evening, Mrs Maloney. How're *you?*'

'I want some potatoes please, Sam. Yes, and I think a can of peas.'

The man turned and reached up behind him on the shelf for the peas.

'Patrick's decided he's tired and doesn't want to eat out tonight,' she told him. 'We usually go out Thursdays, you know, and now he's caught me without any vegetables in the house.'

'Then how about meat, Mrs Maloney?'

'No, I've got meat, thanks. I got a nice leg of lamb, from the freezer.'

'Oh.'

'I don't much like cooking it frozen, Sam, but I'm taking a chance on it this time. You think it'll be all right?'

'Personally,' the grocer said, 'I don't believe it makes any difference. You want these Idaho potatoes?'

'Oh yes, that'll be fine. Two of those.'

'Anything else?' The grocer cocked his head on one side, looking at her pleasantly. 'How about afterwards? What you going to give him for afterwards?'

'Well – what would you suggest, Sam?'

The man glanced around his shop. 'How about a nice big slice of cheesecake? I know he likes that.'

'Perfect,' she said. 'He loves it.'

And when it was all wrapped and she had paid, she put on her brightest smile and said, 'Thank you, Sam. Good night.'

'Good night, Mrs Maloney. And thank you.'

And now, she told herself as she hurried back, all she was doing now, she was returning home to her husband and he was waiting for his supper; and she must cook it good, and make it as tasty as possible because the poor man was tired; and if, when she entered the house, she happened to find anything unusual, or tragic, or terrible, then naturally it would be a shock and she'd become frantic with grief and horror. Mind you, she wasn't *expecting* to find anything. She was just going home with the vegetables. Mrs Patrick Maloney going home with the vegetables on Thursday evening to cook supper for her husband.

That's the way, she told herself. Do everything right and natural. Keep things absolutely natural and there'll be no need for any acting at all.

Therefore, when she entered the kitchen by the back door, she was humming a little tune to herself and smiling.

'Patrick!' she called. 'How are you, darling?'

She put the parcel down on the table and went through into the living-room; and when she saw him lying there on the floor with his legs doubled up and one arm twisted back underneath his body, it really was rather a shock. All the old love and longing for him welled up inside her, and she ran over to him, knelt down beside him, and began to cry her heart out. It was easy. No acting was necessary.

A few minutes later she got up and went to the phone. She knew the number of the police station, and when the man at the other end answered, she cried to him, 'Quick! Come quick! Patrick's dead!'

'Who's speaking?'

'Mrs Maloney. Mrs Patrick Maloney.'

'You mean Patrick Maloney's dead?'

'I think so,' she sobbed. 'He's lying on the floor and I think he's dead.'

'Be right over,' the man said.

The car came very quickly, and when she opened the front door, two policemen walked in. She knew them both – she knew nearly all the men at that precinct – and she fell right into Jack Noonan's arms, weeping hysterically. He put her gently into a chair, then went over to join the other one, who was called O'Malley, kneeling by the body.

'Is he dead?' she cried.

'I'm afraid he is. What happened?'

Briefly, she told her story about going out to the grocer and coming back to find him on the floor. While she was talking, crying and talking, Noonan discovered a small patch of congealed blood on the dead man's head. He showed it to O'Malley who got up at once and hurried to the phone.

Soon, other men began to come into the house. First a doctor, then two detectives, one of whom she knew by name. Later, a police photographer arrived and took pictures, and a man who knew about fingerprints. There was a great deal of whispering and muttering beside the corpse, and the detectives kept asking her a lot of questions. But they always treated her kindly. She told her story again, this time right from the beginning, when Patrick had come in, and she was sewing, and he was tired, so tired he hadn't wanted to go out for supper. She told how she'd put the meat in the oven – 'it's there now, cooking' – and how she'd slipped out to the grocer for vegetables, and come back to find him lying on the floor.

'Which grocer?' one of the detectives asked.

She told him, and he turned and whispered something to the other detective who immediately went outside into the street.

In fifteen minutes he was back with a page of notes, and there was more whispering, and through her sobbing she heard a few of the whispered phrases – '. . . acted quite normal . . . very cheerful . . . wanted to give him a good supper . . . peas . . . cheesecake . . . impossible that she . . .'

After a while, the photographer and the doctor departed and two other men came in and took the corpse away on a stretcher. Then the fingerprint man went away. The two detectives remained, and so did the two policemen. They were exceptionally nice to her, and Jack Noonan asked if she wouldn't rather go somewhere else, to her sister's house perhaps, or to his own wife who would take care of her and put her up for the night.

No, she said. She didn't feel she could move even a yard at the moment. Would they mind awfully if she stayed just where she was until she felt better? She didn't feel too good at the moment, she really didn't.

Then hadn't she better lie down on the bed? Jack Noonan asked.

No, she said, she'd like to stay right where she was, in this chair. A little later perhaps, when she felt better, she would move.

So they left her there while they went about their business, searching the house. Occasionally one of the detectives asked her another question. Sometimes Jack Noonan spoke to her gently as he passed by. Her husband, he told her, had been killed by a blow on the back of the head administered with a heavy blunt instrument, almost certainly a large piece of metal. They were looking for the weapon. The murderer may have taken it with him, but on the other hand he may've thrown it away or hidden it somewhere on the premises.

'It's the old story,' he said. 'Get the weapon, and you've got the man.'

Later, one of the detectives came up and sat beside her. Did she know, he asked, of anything in the house that could've been used as the weapon? Would she mind having a look around to see if anything was missing – a very big spanner, for example, or a heavy metal vase.

They didn't have any heavy metal vases, she said.

'Or a big spanner?'

She didn't think they had a big spanner. But there might be some things like that in the garage.

The search went on. She knew that there were other police-men in the garden all around the house. She could hear their footsteps on the gravel outside, and sometimes she saw the flash of a torch through a chink in the curtains. It began to get late, nearly nine she noticed by the clock on the mantel. The four men searching the rooms seemed to be growing weary, a trifle exasperated.

'Jack,' she said, the next time Sergeant Noonan went by. 'Would you mind giving me a drink?'

'Sure I'll give you a drink. You mean this whisky?'

'Yes, please. But just a small one. It might make me feel

better.'

He handed her the glass.

'Why don't you have one yourself,' she said. 'You must be awfully tired. Please do. You've been very good to me.'

'Well,' he answered. 'It's not strictly allowed, but I might take just a drop to keep me going.'

One by one the others came in and were persuaded to take a little nip of whisky. They stood around rather awkwardly with the drinks in their hands, uncomfortable in her presence, trying to say consoling things to her. Sergeant Noonan wandered into the kitchen, came out quickly and said, 'Look, Mrs Maloney. You know that oven of yours is still on, and the meat still inside.'

'Oh *dear* me!' she cried. 'So it is!'

'I better turn it off for you, hadn't I?'

'Will you do that, Jack. Thank you so much.'

When the sergeant returned the second time, she looked at him with her large, dark, tearful eyes. 'Jack Noonan,' she said.

'Yes?'

'Would you do me a small favour – you and these others?'

'We can try, Mrs Maloney.'

'Well,' she said. 'Here you all are, and good friends of dear Patrick's too, and helping to catch the man who killed him. You must be terrible hungry by now because it's long past your supper time, and I know Patrick would never forgive me, God bless his soul, if I allowed you to remain in his house without offering you decent hospitality. Why don't you eat up that lamb that's in the oven? It'll be cooked just right by now.'

'Wouldn't dream of it,' Sergeant Noonan said.

'Please,' she begged. 'Please eat it. Personally I couldn't touch a thing, certainly not what's been in the house when he was here. But it's all right for you. It'd be a favour to me if you'd eat it up. Then you can go on with your work again afterwards.'

There was a good deal of hesitating among the four police-men, but they were clearly hungry, and in the end they were persuaded to go into the kitchen and help themselves. The woman stayed where she was, listening to them through the open door, and she could hear them speaking among them-selves, their voices thick and sloppy because their mouths were full of meat.

'Have some more, Charlie?'

'No. Better not finish it.'

'She *wants* us to finish it. She said so. Be doing her a favour.'

'Okay then. Give me some more.'

'That's the hell of a big club the guy must've used to hit poor Patrick,' one of them was saying. 'The doc says his skull was smashed all to pieces just like from a sledge-hammer.'

'That's why it ought to be easy to find.'

'Exactly what I say.'

'Whoever done it, they're not going to be carrying a thing like that around with them longer than they need.'

One of them belched.

'Personally, I think it's right here on the premises.'

'Probably right under our very noses. What do you think, Jack?'

And in the other room, Mary Maloney began to giggle.

The Bride Comes to Yellow Sky
STEPHEN CRANE

1

The great Pullman was whirling onward with such dignity of motion that a glance from the window seemed simply to prove that the plains of Texas were pouring eastward. Vast flats of green grass, dull-hued spaces of mesquite and cactus, little groups of frame houses, woods of light and tender trees, all were sweeping into the east, sweeping over the horizon, a precipice.

A newly married pair had boarded this coach at San Antonio. The man's face was reddened from many days in the wind and sun, and a direct result of his new black clothes was that his brick-coloured hands were constantly performing in a most conscious fashion. From time to time he looked down respectfully at his attire. He sat with a hand on each knee, like a man waiting in a barber's shop. The glances he devoted to other passengers were furtive and shy.

The bride was not pretty, nor was she very young. She wore a dress of blue cashmere, with small reservations of velvet here and there, and with steel buttons abounding. She continually twisted her head to regard her puff sleeves, very stiff, straight, and high. They embarrassed her. It was quite apparent that she had cooked, and that she expected to cook, dutifully. The blushes caused by the careless scrutiny of some passengers as she had entered the car were strange to see upon this plain, underclass countenance, which was drawn in placid, almost emotionless lines.

They were evidently very happy. 'Ever been in a parlour-car before?' he asked, smiling with delight.

'No,' she answered; 'I never was. It's fine, ain't it?'

'Great! And then after a while we'll go forward to the diner, and get a big lay-out. Finest meal in the world. Charge a dollar.'

'Oh, do they?' cried the bride. 'Charge a dollar? Why, that's too much – for us – ain't it, Jack?'

'Not this trip, anyhow,' he answered bravely. 'We're going to go the whole thing.'

Later he explained to her about the trains. 'You see, it's a thousand miles from one end of Texas to the other; and this train runs right across it, and never stops but four times.' He had the pride of an owner. He pointed out to her the dazzling fittings of the coach; and in truth her eyes opened wider as she contemplated the sea-green figured velvet, the shining brass, silver, and glass, the wood that gleamed as darkly brilliant as the surface of a pool of oil. At one end a bronze figure sturdily held a support for a separated chamber, and at convenient places on the ceiling were frescos in olive and silver.

To the minds of the pair, their surroundings reflected the glory of their marriage that morning in San Antonio; this was the environment of their new estate; and the man's face in particular beamed with an elation that made him appear ridiculous to the Negro porter. This individual at times surveyed them from afar with an amused and superior grin. On other occasions he bullied them with skill in ways that did not make it exactly plain to them that they were being bullied. He subtly used all the manners of the most unconquerable kind of snobbery. He oppressed them; but of this oppression they had small knowledge, and they speedily forgot that infrequently a number of travellers covered them with stares of derisive enjoyment. Historically there was supposed to be something infinitely humorous in their situation.

'We are due in Yellow Sky at 3.42,' he said, looking tenderly into her eyes.

'Oh, are we?' she said, as if she had not been aware of it. To evince surprise at her husband's statement was part of her wifely amiability. She took from a pocket a little silver watch; and as she held it before her, and stared at it with a frown of attention, the new husband's face shone.

'I bought it in San Anton' from a friend of mine,' he told her gleefully.

'It's seventeen minutes past twelve,' she said, looking up at him with a kind of shy and clumsy coquetry. A passenger, noting this play, grew excessively sardonic, and winked at himself in one of the numerous mirrors.

At last they went to the dining-car. Two rows of negro waiters, in glowing white suits, surveyed their entrance with

60

interest, and also the equanimity, of men who had been fore-warned. The pair fell to the lot of a waiter who happened to feel pleasure in steering them through their meal. He viewed them with the manner of a fatherly pilot, his countenance radiant with benevolence. The patronage, entwined with the ordinary deference, was not plain to them. And yet, as they returned to their coach, they showed in their faces a sense of escape.

To the left, miles down a long purple slope, was a little ribbon of mist where moved the keening Rio Grande. The train was approaching it at an angle, and the apex was Yellow Sky. Presently it was apparent that, as the distance from Yellow Sky grew shorter, the husband became commensurately restless. His brick-red hands were more insistent in their prominence. Occasionally he was even rather absent-minded and far-away when the bride leaned forward and addressed him.

As a matter of truth, Jack Potter was beginning to find the shadow of a deed weigh upon him like a leaden slab. He, the town marshal of Yellow Sky, a man known, liked, and feared in his corner, a prominent person, had gone to San Antonio to meet a girl he believed he loved, and there, after the usual prayers, had actually induced her to marry him, without consulting Yellow Sky for any part of the transaction. He was now bringing his bride before an innocent and unsuspecting community.

Of course people in Yellow Sky married as it pleased them, in accordance with a general custom; but such was Potter's thought of his duty to his friends, or of their idea of his duty, or of an unspoken form which does not control men in these matters, that he felt he was heinous. He had committed an extraordinary crime. Face to face with this girl in San Antonio, and spurred by his sharp impulse, he had gone headlong over all the social hedges. At San Antonio he was like a man hidden in the dark. A knife to sever any friendly duty, any form, was easy to his hand in that remote city. But the hour of Yellow Sky – the hour of daylight – was approaching.

He knew full well that his marriage was an important thing to his town. It could only be exceeded by the burning of the new hotel. His friends could not forgive him. Frequently he had reflected on the advisability of telling them by telegraph, but a new cowardice had been upon him. He feared to do it. And now the train was hurrying him toward a scene of amazement, glee, and reproach. He glanced out of the window at the line of haze swinging slowly in toward the train.

Yellow Sky had a kind of brass band, which played painfully, to the delight of the populace. He laughed without heart as he thought of it. If the citizens could dream of his prospective arrival with his bride, they would parade the band at the station and escort them, amid cheers and laughing congratulations, to his adobe home.

He resolved that he would use all the devices of speed and plainscraft in making the journey from the station to his house. Once within that safe citadel, he could issue some sort of vocal bulletin, and then not go among the citizens until they had time to wear off a little of their enthusiasm.

The bride looked anxiously at him. 'What's worrying you, Jack?'

He laughed again. 'I'm not worrying, girl; I'm only thinking of Yellow Sky.'

She flushed in comprehension.

A sense of mutual guilt invaded their minds and developed a finer tenderness. They looked at each other with eyes softly aglow. But Potter often laughed the same nervous laugh; the flush upon the bride's face seemed quite permanent.

The traitor to the feelings of Yellow Sky narrowly watched the speeding landscape. 'We're nearly there,' he said.

Presently the porter came and announced the proximity of Potter's home. He held a brush in his hand, and, with all his airy superiority gone, he brushed Potter's new clothes as the latter slowly turned this way and that way. Potter fumbled out a coin and gave it to the porter, as he had seen others do. It was a heavy and muscle-bound business, as that of a man shoeing his first horse.

The porter took their bag, and as the train began to slow they moved forward to the hooded platform of the car. Presently the two engines and their long string of coaches rushed into the station of Yellow Sky.

'They have to take water here,' said Potter, from a constricted throat and in mournful cadence, as one announcing death. Before the train stopped his eye had swept the length of the platform, and he was glad and astonished to see there was none upon it but the station-agent, who, with a slightly hurried and anxious air, was walking toward the water-tanks. When the train had halted, the porter alighted first, and placed in position a little temporary step.

'Come on, girl,' said Potter, hoarsely. As he helped her down they each laughed on a false note. He took the bag from the Negro, and bade his wife cling to his arm. As they slunk rapidly away, his hang-dog glance perceived that they were unloading the two trunks, and also that the station-agent, far ahead near the baggage-car, had turned and was running toward him, making gestures. He laughed, and groaned as he laughed, when he noted the first effect of his marital bliss upon Yellow Sky. He gripped his wife's arm firmly to his side, and they fled. Behind them the porter stood, chuckling fatuously.

2

The California express on the Southern Railway was due at Yellow Sky in twenty-one minutes. There were six men at the bar of the Weary Gentleman saloon. One was a drummer who talked a great deal and rapidly; three were Texans who did not care to talk at that time; and two were Mexican sheepherders, who did not talk as a general practice in the Weary Gentleman saloon. The bar-keeper's dog lay on the board walk that crossed in front of the door. His head was on his paws, and he glanced drowsily here and there with the constant vigilance of a dog that is kicked on occasion. Across the sandy street were some vivid green grass-plots, so wonderful in appearance, amid the sands that burned near them in a blazing sun, that they caused a doubt in the mind. They exactly resembled the grass mats used to represent lawns on the stage. At the cooler end of the railway station, a man without a coat sat in a tilted chair and smoked his pipe. The fresh-cut bank of the Rio Grande circled near the town, and there could be seen beyond it a great plum-coloured plain of mesquite.

Save for the busy drummer and his companions in the saloon, Yellow Sky was dozing. The newcomer leaned gracefully upon the bar, and recited many tales with the confidence of a bard who has come upon a new field.

'— and at the moment that the old man fell downstairs with the bureau in his arms, the old woman was coming up with two scuttles of coal, and of course —'

The drummer's tale was interrupted by a young man who suddenly appeared in the open door. He cried: 'Scratchy Wilson's drunk, and has turned loose with both hands.' The two Mexicans at once set down their glasses and faded out of the rear entrance of the saloon.

The drummer, innocent and jocular, answered: 'All right, old man. S'pose he has? Come in and have a drink, anyhow.'

But the information had made such an obvious cleft in every skull in the room that the drummer was obliged to see its importance. All had become instantly solemn. 'Say,' said he, mystified, 'what is this?' His three companions made the introductory gesture of eloquent speech; but the young man at the door forestalled them.

'It means, my friend,' he answered, as he came into the saloon, 'that for the next two hours this town won't be a health resort.'

The barkeeper went to the door, and locked and barred it; reaching out of the window, he pulled in heavy wooden shutters, and barred them. Immediately a solemn, chapel-like gloom was upon the place. The drummer was looking from one to another.

'But say,' he cried, 'what is this, anyhow? You don't mean there is going to be a gun-fight?'

'Don't know whether there'll be a fight or not,' answered one man, grimly; 'but there'll be some shootin' – some good shootin'.'

The young man who had warned them waved his hand. 'Oh, there'll be a fight fast enough, if any one wants it. Anybody can get a fight out there in the street. There's a fight just waiting.'

The drummer seemed to be swayed between the interest of a foreigner and a perception of personal danger.

'What did you say his name was?' he asked.

'Scratchy Wilson,' they answered in chorus.

'And will he kill anybody? What are you going to do? Does this happen often? Does he rampage around like this once a week or so? Can he break in that door?'

'No; he can't break down that door,' replied the barkeeper. 'He's tried it three times. But when he comes you'd better lay down on the floor, stranger. He's dead sure to shoot at it, and a bullet may come through.'

Thereafter the drummer kept a strict eye upon the door. The time had not yet been called for him to hug the floor, but, as a minor precaution, he sidled near to the wall. 'Will he kill anybody?' he said again.

The men laughed low and scornfully at the question.

'He's out to shoot, and he's out for trouble. Don't see any good in experimentin' with him.'

'But what do you do in a case like this? What do you do?'

A man responded: 'Why, he and Jack Potter –'

'But,' in chorus the other men interrupted, 'Jack Potter's in San Anton'.'

'Well, who is he? What's he got to do with it?'

'Oh, he's the town marshal. He goes out and fights Scratchy when he gets on one of these tears.'

'Wow!' said the drummer, mopping his brow. 'Nice job he's got.'

The voices had toned away to mere whisperings. The drummer wished to ask further questions, which were born of an increasing anxiety and bewilderment; but when he attempted them, the men merely looked at him in irritation and motioned him to remain silent. A tense waiting hush was upon them. In the deep shadows of the room their eyes shone as they listened for sounds from the street. One man made three gestures at the barkeeper; and the latter, moving like a ghost, handed him a glass and a bottle. The man poured a full glass of whisky, and set down the bottle noiselessly. He gulped the whisky in a swallow, and turned again toward the door in immovable silence. The drummer saw that the barkeeper, without a sound, had taken a Winchester from beneath the bar. Later he saw this individual beckoning to him, so he tiptoed across the room.

'You better come with me back of the bar.'

'No, thanks,' said the drummer, perspiring; 'I'd rather be where I can make a break for the back door.'

Whereupon the man of bottles made a kindly but peremptory gesture. The drummer obeyed it, and, finding himself seated on a box with his head below the level of the bar, balm was laid upon his soul at sight of various zinc and copper fittings that bore a resemblance to armour-plate. The barkeeper took a seat comfortably upon an adjacent box.

'You see,' he whispered, 'this here Scratchy Wilson is a

wonder with a gun – a perfect wonder; and when he goes on the war-trail, we hunt our holes – naturally. He's about the last one of the old gang that used to hang out along the river here. He's a terror when he's drunk. When he's sober he's all right – kind of simple – wouldn't hurt a fly – nicest fellow in town. But when he's drunk – whoo!'

There were periods of stillness. 'I wish Jack Potter was back from San Anton',' said the barkeeper. 'He shot Wilson up once in the leg – and he would sail in and pull out the kinks in this thing.'

Presently they heard from a distance the sound of a shot, followed by three wild yowls. It instantly removed a bond from the men in the darkened saloon. There was a shuffling of feet. They looked at each other. 'Here he comes,' they said.

3

A man in a maroon-coloured flannel shirt, which had been purchased for purposes of decoration, and made principally by some Jewish women on the East Side of New York, rounded a corner and walked into the middle of the main street of Yellow Sky. In either hand the man held a long, heavy, blue-black revolver. Often he yelled, and these cries rang through a semblance of a deserted village, shrilly flying over the roofs in a volume that seemed to have no relation to the ordinary vocal strength of a man. It was as if the surrounding stillness formed the arch of a tomb over him. These cries of ferocious challenge rang against the walls of silence. And his boots had red tops with gilded imprints, of the kind beloved in winter by little sledding boys on the hillsides of New England.

The man's face flamed in a rage begot of whisky. His eyes, rolling, and yet keen for ambush, hunted the still doorways and windows. He walked with the creeping movement of the midnight cat. As it occurred to him, he roared menacing information. The long revolvers in his hands were as easy as straws; they were moved with an electric swiftness. The little fingers of each hand played sometimes in a musician's way. Plain from the low collar of the shirt, the cords of his neck straightened and sank, straightened and sank, as passion moved him. The only sounds were his terrible invitations. The calm adobes preserved their demeanour at the passing of this small thing in the middle of the street.

There was no offer of fight – no offer of fight. The man called to the sky. There were no attractions. He bellowed and fumed and swayed his revolvers here and everywhere.

The dog of the barkeeper of the Weary Gentleman saloon had not appreciated the advance of events. He yet lay dozing in front of his master's door. At sight of the dog, the man paused and raised his revolver humorously. At sight of the man, the dog sprang up and walked diagonally away, with a sullen head, and growling. The man yelled, and the dog broke into a gallop. As it was about to enter an alley, there was a loud noise, a whistling, and something spat the ground directly before it. The dog screamed, and, wheeling in terror, galloped headlong in a new direction. Again there was a noise, a whistling, and sand was kicked viciously before it. Fear-stricken, the dog turned and flurried like an animal in a pen. The man stood laughing, his weapons at his hips.

Ultimately the man was attracted by the closed door of the Weary Gentleman saloon. He went to it and, hammering with a revolver, demanded drink.

The door remaining imperturbable, he picked a bit of paper from the walk, and nailed it to the framework with a knife. He then turned his back contemptuously upon this popular resort and, walking to the opposite side of the street and spinning there on his heel quickly and lithely, fired at the bit of paper. He missed it by a half-inch. He swore at himself, and went away. Later he comfortably fusilladed the windows of his most intimate friend. The man was playing with this town; it was a toy for him.

But still there was no offer of fight. The name of Jack Potter, his ancient antagonist, entered his mind, and he concluded that it would be a glad thing if he should go to Potter's house, and by bombardment induce him to come out and fight. He moved in the direction of his desire, chanting Apache scalp-music.

When he arrived at it, Potter's house presented the same still front as had the other adobes. Taking up a strategic position, the man howled a challenge. But this house regarded him as might a great stone god. It gave no sign. After a decent wait, the man howled further challenges, mingling with them wonderful epithets.

Presently there came the spectacle of a man churning himself into deepest rage over the immobility of a house. He fumed at it as the winter wind attacks a prairie cabin in the North. To the distance there should have gone the sound of a tumult like the fighting of two hundred Mexicans. As necessity bade him, he paused for breath or to reload his revolvers.

4

Potter and his bride walked sheepishly and with speed. Sometimes they laughed together shamefacedly and low.

'Next corner, dear,' he said finally.

They put forth the efforts of a pair walking bowed against a strong wind. Potter was about to raise a finger to point the first appearance of the new home when, as they circled the corner, they came face to face with a man in a maroon-coloured shirt, who was feverishly pushing cartridges into a large revolver. Upon the instant the man dropped his revolver to the ground and, like lightning, whipped another from its holster. The second weapon was aimed at the bridegroom's chest.

There was a silence. Potter's mouth seemed to be merely a grave for his tongue. He exhibited an instinct to at once loosen his arm from the woman's grip, and he dropped the bag to the sand. As for the bride, her face had gone as yellow as old cloth. She was a slave to hideous rites, gazing at the apparitional snake.

The two men faced each other at a distance of three paces. He of the revolver smiled with a new and quiet ferocity.

'Tried to sneak up on me,' he said. 'Tried to sneak up on me!' His eyes grew more baleful. As Potter made a slight movement, the man thrust his revolver venomously forward. 'No; don't you do it, Jack Potter. Don't you move a finger toward a gun just yet. Don't you move an eyelash. The time has come for me to settle with you, and I'm goin' to do it my own way, and loaf along with no interferin'. So if you don't want a gun bent on you, just mind what I tell you.'

Potter looked at his enemy. 'I ain't got a gun on me, Scratchy,' he said. 'Honest, I ain't.' He was stiffening and steadying, but yet somewhere at the back of his mind a vision of the Pullman floated: the sea-green figured velvet, the shining brass, silver, and glass, the wood that gleamed as darkly brilliant as the surface of a pool of oil – all the glory of the marriage, the environment of the new estate. 'You know I fight when it comes to fighting, Scratchy Wilson; but I ain't got a gun on me. You'll have to do all the shootin' yourself.'

His enemy's face went livid. He stepped forward, and lashed his weapon to and fro before Potter's chest. 'Don't you tell me you ain't got no gun on you, you whelp. Don't tell me no lie like that. There ain't a man in Texas ever seen you without no gun. Don't take me for no kid.' His eyes blazed with light, and his throat worked like a pump.

'I ain't takin' you for no kid,' answered Potter. His heels had not moved an inch backward. 'I'm takin' you for a damn fool. I tell you I ain't got a gun, and I ain't. If you're goin' to shoot me up, you better begin now; you'll never get a chance like this again.'

So much enforced reasoning had told on Wilson's rage; he was calmer. 'If you ain't got a gun, why ain't you got a gun?' he sneered. 'Been to Sunday-school?'

'I ain't got a gun because I've just come from San Anton' with my wife. I'm married,' said Potter. 'And if I'd thought there was going to be any galoots like you prowling around when I brought my wife home, I'd had a gun, and don't you forget it.'

'Married!' said Scratchy, not at all comprehending.

'Yes, married. I'm married,' said Potter, distinctly.

'Married?' said Scratchy. Seemingly for the first time, he saw the drooping, drowning woman at the other man's side. 'No!' he said. He was like a creature allowed a glimpse of another world. He moved a pace backward, and his arm, with the revolver, dropped to his side. 'Is this the lady?' he asked.

'Yes; this is the lady,' answered Potter.

There was another period of silence.

'Well,' said Wilson at last, slowly, 'I s'pose it's all off now.'

'It's all off if you say so, Scratchy. You know I didn't make the trouble.' Potter lifted his valise.

'Well, I 'low it's off, Jack,' said Wilson. He was looking at the ground. 'Married!' He was not a student of chivalry; it was merely that in the presence of this foreign condition he was a simple child of the earlier plains. He picked up his starboard revolver, and, placing both weapons in their holsters, he went away. His feet made funnel-shaped tracks in the heavy sand.

Wine on the Desert

MAX BRAND

There was no hurry, except for the thirst, like clotted salt, in the back of his throat, and Durante rode on slowly, rather enjoying the last moments of dryness before he reached the cold water in Tony's house. There was really no hurry at all. He had almost twenty-four hours' head start, for they would not find his dead man until this morning. After that, there would be perhaps several hours of delay before the sheriff gathered a sufficient posse and started on his trail. Or perhaps the sheriff would be fool enough to come alone.

Durante had been able to see the wheel and fan of Tony's windmill for more than an hour, but he could not make out the ten acres of the vineyard until he had topped the last rise, for the vines had been planted in a hollow. The lowness of the ground, Tony used to say, accounted for the water that gathered in the well during the wet season. The rains sank through the desert sand, through the gravels beneath, and gathered in a bowl of clay hardpan far below.

In the middle of the rainless season the well ran dry but, long before that, Tony had every drop of the water pumped up into a score of tanks made of cheap corrugated iron. Slender pipe lines carried the water from the tanks to the vines and from time to time let them sip enough life to keep them until the winter darkened overhead suddenly, one November day, and the rain came down, and all the earth made a great hushing sound as it drank. Durante had heard that whisper of drinking when he was here before; but he never had seen the place in the middle of the long drought.

The windmill looked like a sacred emblem to Durante, and the twenty stodgy, tar-painted tanks blessed his eyes; but a heavy sweat broke out at once from his body. For the air of the hollow, unstirred by wind, was hot and still as a bowl of soup. A reddish soup. The vines were powdered with thin red dust, also. They were wretched, dying things to look at, for the grapes had been gathered, the new wine had been made, and now the leaves hung in ragged tatters.

70

Durante rode up to the squat adobe house and right through the entrance into the patio. A flowering vine clothed three sides of the little court. Durante did not know the name of the plant, but it had large white blossoms with golden hearts that poured sweetness on the air. Durante hated the sweetness. It made him more thirsty.

He threw the reins of his mule and strode into the house. The water cooler stood in the hall outside the kitchen. There were two jars made of a porous stone, very ancient things, and the liquid which distilled through the pores kept the contents cool. The jar on the left held water; that on the right contained wine. There was a big tin dipper hanging on a peg beside each jar. Durante tossed off the cover of the vase on the left and plunged it in until the delicious coolness closed well above his wrist.

'Hey, Tony,' he called. Out of his dusty throat the cry was a mere groaning. He drank and called again, clearly, 'Tony!'

A voice pealed from the distance.

Durante, pouring down the second dipper of water, smelled the alkali dust which had shaken off his own clothes. It seemed to him that heat was radiating like light from his clothes, from his body, and the cool dimness of the house was soaking it up. He heard the wooden leg of Tony bumping on the ground, and Durante grinned; then Tony came in with that hitch and sideswing with which he accommodated the stiffness of his artificial leg. His brown face shone with sweat as though a special ray of light were focused on it.

'Ah, Dick!' he said. 'Good old Dick! . . . How long since you came last! . . . Wouldn't Julia be glad! Wouldn't she be glad!'

'Ain't she here?' asked Durante, jerking his head suddenly away from the dripping dipper.

'She's away at Nogalez,' said Tony. 'It gets so hot. I said, "You go up to Nogalez, Julia, where the wind don't forget to blow." She cried, but I made her go.'

'Did she cry?' asked Durante.

'Julia . . . that's a good girl,' said Tony.

'Yeah. You bet she's good,' said Durante. He put the dipper quickly to his lips but did not swallow for a moment; he was grinning too widely. Afterward he said: 'You wouldn't throw some water into that mule of mine, would you, Tony?'

71

Tony went out with his wooden leg clumping loud on the wooden floor, softly in the patio dust. Durante found the hammock in the corner of the patio. He lay down in it and watched the colour of sunset flush the mists of desert dust that rose to the zenith. The water was soaking through his body; hunger began, and then the rattling of pans in the kitchen and the cheerful cry of Tony's voice:

'What you want, Dick? I got some pork. You don't want pork. I'll make you some good Mexican beans. Hot. Ah ha, I know that old Dick. I have plenty of good wine for you, Dick. Tortillas. Even Julia can't make tortillas like me. . . . And what about a nice young rabbit?'

'All blowed full of buckshot?' growled Durante.

'No, no. I kill them with the rifle.'

'You kill rabbits with a rifle?' repeated Durante, with a quick interest.

'It's the only gun I have,' said Tony. 'If I catch them in the sights, they are dead. . . . A wooden leg cannot walk very far. . . . I must kill them quick. You see? They come close to the house about sunrise and flop their ears. I shoot through the head.'

'Yeah? Yeah?' muttered Durante. 'Through the head?' He relaxed, scowling. He passed his hand over his face, over his head.

Then Tony began to bring the food out into the patio and lay it on a small wooden table; a lantern hanging against the wall of the house included the table in a dim half circle of light. They sat there and ate. Tony had scrubbed himself for the meal. His hair was soaked in water and sleeked back over his round skull. A man in the desert might be willing to pay five dollars for as much water as went to the soaking of that hair.

Everything was good. Tony knew how to cook, and he knew how to keep the glasses filled with his wine.

'This is old wine. This is my father's wine. Eleven years old,' said Tony. 'You look at the light through it. You see that brown in the red? That's the soft that time puts in good wine, my father always said.'

'What killed your father?' asked Durante.

Tony lifted his hand as though he were listening or as though he were pointing out a thought.

'The desert killed him. I found his mule. It was dead, too.

There was a leak in the canteen. My father was only five miles away when the buzzards showed him to me.'

'Five miles? Just an hour. . . . Good Lord!' said Durante. He stared with big eyes. 'Just dropped down and died?' he asked.

'No,' said Tony. 'When you die of thirst, you always die just one way. . . . First you tear off your shirt, then your undershirt. That's to be cooler. . . . And the sun comes and cooks your bare skin. . . . And then you think . . . there is water everywhere, if you dig down far enough. You begin to dig. The dust comes up your nose. You start screaming. You break your nails in the sand. You wear the flesh off the tips of your fingers, to the bone.' He took a quick swallow of wine.

'Without you seen a man die of thirst, how d'you know they start to screaming?' asked Durante.

'They got a screaming look when you find them,' said Tony. 'Take some more wine. The desert never can get to you here. My father showed me the way to keep the desert away from the hollow. We live pretty good here? No?'

'Yeah,' said Durante, loosening his shirt collar. 'Yeah, pretty good.'

Afterward he slept well in the hammock until the report of a rifle waked him and he saw the colour of dawn in the sky. It was such a great, round bowl that for a moment he felt as though he were above, looking down into it.

He got up and saw Tony coming in holding a rabbit by the ears, the rifle in his other hand.

'You see?' said Tony. 'Breakfast came and called on us!' He laughed.

Durante examined the rabbit with care. It was nice and fat and it had been shot through the head. Through the middle of the head. Such a shudder went down the back of Durante that he washed gingerly before breakfast; he felt that his blood was cooled for the entire day.

It was a good breakfast, too, with flapjacks and stewed rabbit with green peppers, and a quart of strong coffee. Before they had finished, the sun struck through the east window and started them sweating.

'Gimme a look at that rifle of yours, Tony, will you?' Durante asked.

'You take a look at my rifle, but don't you steal the luck that's in it,' laughed Tony. He brought the fifteen-shot Winchester.

'Loaded right to the brim?' asked Durante.

'I always load it full the minute I get back home,' said Tony.

'Tony, come outside with me,' commanded Durante.

They went out from the house. The sun turned the sweat of Durante to hot water and then dried his skin so that his clothes felt transparent.

'Tony, I gotta be damn mean,' said Durante. 'Stand right there where I can see you. Don't try to get close. . . . Now listen. . . . The sheriff's gunna be along this trail sometime today, looking for me. He'll load up himself and all his gang with water out of your tanks. Then he'll follow my sign across the desert. Get me? He'll follow if he finds water on the place. But he's not gunna find water.'

'What you done, poor Dick?' said Tony. 'Now look. . . . I could hide you in the old wine cellar where nobody . . .'

'The sheriff's not gunna find any water,' said Durante. 'It's gunna be like this.'

He put the rifle to his shoulder, aimed, fired. The shot struck the base of the nearest tank, ranging down through the bottom. A semicircle of darkness began to stain the soil near the edge of the iron wall.

Tony fell on his knees. 'No, no, Dick! Good Dick!' he said. 'Look! All the vineyard. It will die. It will turn into old, dead wood. Dick . . .'

'Shut your face,' said Durante. 'Now I've started, I kinda like the job.'

Tony fell on his face and put his hands over his ears. Durante drilled a bullet hole through the tanks, one after another. Afterward, he leaned on the rifle.

'Take my canteen and go and fill it with water out of the cooling jar,' he said. 'Snap into it, Tony!'

Tony got up. He raised the canteen and looked around him, not at the tanks from which the water was pouring so that the noise of the earth drinking was audible, but at the rows of his vineyard. Then he went into the house.

Durante mounted his mule. He shifted the rifle to his left hand and drew out the heavy Colt from its holster. Tony came dragging back to him, his head down. Durante watched Tony

74

with a careful revolver but he gave up the canteen without lifting his eyes.

'The trouble with you, Tony,' said Durante, 'is you're yellow. I'd of fought a tribe of wildcats with my bare hands before I'd let 'em do what I'm doin' to you. But you sit back and take it.'

Tony did not seem to hear. He stretched out his hands to the vines.

'Ah, my God,' said Tony. 'Will you let them all die?'

Durante shrugged his shoulders. He shook the canteen to make sure that it was full. It was so brimming that there was hardly room for the liquid to make a sloshing sound. Then he turned the mule and kicked it into a dogtrot.

Half a mile from the house of Tony, he threw the empty rifle to the ground. There was no sense packing that useless weight, and Tony with his peg leg would hardly come this far.

Durante looked back, a mile or so later, and saw the little image of Tony picking up the rifle from the dust, then staring earnestly after his guest. Durante remembered the neat little hole clipped through the head of the rabbit. Wherever he went, his trail never could return again to the vineyard in the desert. But then, commencing to picture to himself the arrival of the sweating sheriff and his posse at the house of Tony, Durante laughed heartily.

The sheriff's posse could get plenty of wine, of course, but without water a man could not hope to make the desert voyage, even with a mule or a horse to help him on the way. Durante patted the full, rounding side of his canteen. He might even now begin with the first sip but it was a luxury to postpone pleasure until desire became greater.

He raised his eyes along the trail. Close by, it was merely dotted with occasional bones, but distance joined the dots into an unbroken chalk line which wavered with a strange leisure across the Apache Desert, pointing toward the cool blue promise of the mountains. The next morning he would be among them.

A coyote whisked out of a gully and ran like a grey puff of dust on the wind. His tongue hung out like a little red rag from the side of his mouth; and suddenly Durante was dry to the marrow. He uncorked and lifted his canteen. It had a slightly sour smell; perhaps the sacking which covered it had grown a

trifle old. And then he poured a great mouthful of lukewarm liquid. He had swallowed it before his senses could give him warning.

It was wine.

He looked first of all toward the mountains. They were as calmly blue, as distant as when he had started that morning. Twenty-four hours not on water, but on wine.

'I deserve it,' said Durante. 'I trusted him to fill the canteen. . . . I deserve it. Curse him!' With a mighty resolution, he quieted the panic in his soul. He would not touch the stuff until noon. Then he would take one discreet sip. He would win through.

Hours went by. He looked at his watch and found it was only ten o'clock. And he had thought that it was on the verge of noon! He uncorked the wine and drank freely and, corking the canteen, felt almost as though he needed a drink of water more than before. He sloshed the contents of the canteen. Already it was horribly light.

Once, he turned the mule and considered the return trip; but he could remember the head of the rabbit too clearly, drilled right through the centre. The vineyard, the rows of old twisted, gnarled little trunks with the bark peeling off . . . every vine was to Tony like a human life. And Durante had condemned them all to death.

He faced the blue of the mountains again. His heart raced in his breast with terror. Perhaps it was fear and not the suction of that dry and deadly air that made his tongue cleave to the roof of his mouth.

The day grew old. Nausea began to work in his stomach, nausea alternating with sharp pains. When he looked down, he saw that there was blood on his boots. He had been spurring the mule until the red ran down from its flanks. It went with a curious stagger, like a rocking horse with a broken rocker; and Durante grew aware that he had been keeping the mule at a gallop for a long time. He pulled it to a halt. It stood with wide-braced legs. Its head was down. When he leaned from the saddle, he saw that its mouth was open.

'It's gunna die,' said Durante. 'It's gunna die . . . what a fool I been . . .'

The mule did not die until after sunset. Durante left everything except his revolver. He packed the weight of that for an

77

hour and discarded it, in turn. His knees were growing weak. When he looked up at the stars, they shone white and clear for a moment only, and then whirled into little racing circles and scrawls of red.

He lay down. He kept his eyes closed and waited for the shaking to go out of his body, but it would not stop. And every breath of darkness was like an inhalation of black dust.

He got up and went on, staggering. Sometimes he found himself running.

Before you die of thirst, you go mad. He kept remembering that. His tongue had swollen big. Before it choked him, if he lanced it with his knife the blood would help him; he would be able to swallow. Then he remembered that the taste of blood is salty.

Once, in his boyhood, he had ridden through a pass with his father and they had looked down on the sapphire of a mountain lake, a hundred thousand million tons of water as cold as snow . . .

When he looked up, now, there were no stars; and this frightened him terribly. He never had seen a desert night so dark. His eyes were failing, he was being blinded. When the morning came, he would not be able to see the mountains, and he would walk around and around in a circle until he dropped and died.

No stars, no wind; the air as still as the waters of a stale pool, and he in the dregs at the bottom . . .

He seized his shirt at the throat and tore it away so that it hung in two rags from his hips.

He could see the earth only well enough to stumble on the rocks. But there were no stars in the heavens. He was blind: he had no more hope than a rat in a well. Ah, but Italian devils know how to put poison in wine that steal all the senses or any one of them: and Tony had chosen to blind Durante.

He heard a sound like water. It was the swishing of the soft deep sand through which he was treading; sand so soft that a man could dig it away with his bare hands. . . .

Afterward, after many hours, out of the blind face of that sky the rain began to fall. It made first a whispering and then a delicate murmur like voices conversing, but after that, just at the dawn, it roared like the hoofs of ten thousand charging horses. Even through that thundering confusion the big birds with naked heads and red, raw necks found their way down to one place in the Apache Desert.

A Mild Attack of Locusts

DORIS LESSING

The rains that year were good, they were coming nicely just as the crops needed them – or so Margaret gathered when the men said they were not too bad. She never had an opinion of her own on matters like the weather, because even to know about what seems a simple thing like the weather needs experience. Which Margaret had not got. The men were Richard her husband, and old Stephen, Richard's father, a farmer from way back, and these two might argue for hours whether the rains were ruinous, or just ordinarily exasperating. Margaret had been on the farm three years. She still did not understand how they did not go bankrupt altogether, when the men never had a good word for the weather, or the soil, or the Government. But she was getting to learn the language. Farmer's language. And they neither went bankrupt nor got very rich. They jogged along, doing comfortably.

Their crop was maize. Their farm was three thousand acres on the ridges that rise up towards the Zambesi escarpment, high, dry windswept country, cold and dusty in winter, but now, being the wet season, steamy with the heat rising in wet soft waves off miles of green foliage. Beautiful it was, with the sky blue and brilliant halls of air, and the bright green folds and hollows of country beneath, and the mountains lying sharp and bare twenty miles off across the rivers. The sky made her eyes ache, she was not used to it. One does not look so much at the sky in the city she came from. So that evening when Richard said: 'The Government is sending out warnings that locusts are expected, coming down from the breeding grounds up North,' her instinct was to look about her at the trees. Insects – swarms of them – horrible! But Richard and the old man had raised their eyes and were looking up over the mountains. 'We haven't had locusts in seven years,' they said. 'They go in cycles, locusts do.' And then: 'There goes our crop for this season!'

But they went on with the work of the farm just as usual, until one day they were coming up the road to the homestead

80

for the midday break, when old Stephen stopped, raised his finger and pointed: 'Look, look, there they are!'

Out ran Margaret to join them, looking at the hills. Out came the servants from the kitchen. They all stood and gazed. Over the rocky levels of the mountain was a streak of rust-coloured air. Locusts. There they came.

At once Richard shouted at the cook-boy. Old Stephen yelled at the house-boy. The cook-boy ran to beat the old plough-share hanging from a tree-branch, which was used to summon the labourers at moments of crisis. The house-boy ran off to the store to collect tin cans, any old bit of metal. The farm was ringing with the clamour of the gong, and they could see the labourers come pouring out of the compound, pointing at the hills and shouting excitedly. Soon they had all come up to the house, and Richard and old Stephen were giving them orders – Hurry, hurry, hurry.

And off they ran again, the two white men with them, and in a few minutes Margaret could see the smoke of fires rising from all around the farm-lands. Piles of wood and grass had been prepared there. There were seven patches of bared soil, yellow and ox-blood colour, and pink, where the new mealies were just showing, making a film of bright green, and around each drifted up thick clouds of smoke. They were throwing wet leaves on to the fires now, to make it acrid and black. Margaret was watching the hills. Now there was a long low cloud advancing, rust-colour still, swelling forwards and out as she looked. The telephone was ringing. Neighbours – quick, quick, there come the locusts. Old Smith had had his crop eaten to the ground. Quick, get your fires started. For of course, while every farmer hoped the locusts would overlook his farm and go on to the next, it was only fair to warn each other, one must play fair. Everywhere, fifty miles over the countryside, the smoke was rising from myriads of fires. Margaret answered the telephone calls, and between stood watching the locusts. The air was darkening. A strange dark-ness, for the sun was blazing – it was like the darkness of a veld fire, when the air gets thick with smoke. The sunlight comes down distorted, a thick hot orange. Oppressive it was, too, with the heaviness of a storm. The locusts were coming fast. Now half the sky was darkened. Behind the reddish veils in front which were the advance guards of the swarm, the main swarm showed in dense black cloud, reaching almost to the sun itself.

Margaret was wondering what she could do to help. She did not know. Then up came old Stephen from the lands. 'We're finished, Margaret, finished! These beggars can eat every leaf and blade off the farm in half an hour! And it is only early afternoon – if we can make enough smoke, make enough noise till the sun goes down, they'll settle somewhere else perhaps. . . .' And then: 'Get the kettle going. It's thirsty work, this.'

So Margaret went to the kitchen, and stoked up the fire, and boiled the water. Now, on the tin roof of the kitchen she could hear the thuds and bangs of falling locusts, or a scratching slither as one skidded down. Here were the first of them. From down on the lands came the beating and banging and clanging of a hundred petrol tins and bits of metal. Stephen impatiently waited while one petrol tin was filled with tea, hot, sweet and orange-coloured, and the other with water. In the meantime, he told Margaret about how twenty years back he was eaten out, made bankrupt by the locust armies. And then, still talking, he hoisted up the petrol cans, one in each hand, by the wood pieces set corner-wise each, and jogged off down to the road to the thirsty labourers. By now the locusts were falling like hail on to the roof of the kitchen. It sounded like a heavy storm. Margaret looked out and saw the air dark with a criss-cross of the insects, and she set her teeth and ran out into it – what the men could do, she could. Overhead the air was thick, locusts everywhere. The locusts were flopping against her, and she brushed them off, heavy red-brown creatures, looking at her with their beady old-men's eyes while they clung with hard serrated legs. She held her breath with disgust and ran into the house. There it was even more like being in a heavy storm. The iron roof was reverberating, and the clamour of iron from the lands was like thunder. Looking out, all the trees were queer and still, clotted with insects, their boughs weighed to the ground. The earth seemed to be moving, locusts crawling everywhere, she could not see the lands at all, so thick was the swarm. Towards the mountains it was like looking into driving rain – even as she watched, the sun was blotted out with a fresh onrush of them. It was a half-night, a perverted blackness. Then came a sharp crack from the bush – a branch

83

had snapped off. Then another. A tree down the slope leaned over and settled heavily to the ground. Through the hail of insects a man came running. More tea, more water was needed. She supplied them. She kept the fires stoked and filled tins with liquid, and then it was four in the afternoon, and the locusts had been pouring across overhead for a couple of hours. Up came old Stephen again, crunching locusts underfoot with every step, locusts clinging all over him, cursing and swearing, banging with his old hat at the air. At the doorway he stopped briefly, hastily pulling at the clinging insects and throwing them off, then he plunged into the locust-free living-room.

'All the crops finished. Nothing left,' he said.

But the gongs were still beating, the men still shouting, and Margaret asked: 'Why do you go on with it, then?'

'The main swarm isn't settling. They are heavy with eggs. They are looking for a place to settle and lay. If we can stop the main body settling on our farm, that's everything. If they get a chance to lay their eggs, we are going to have everything eaten flat with hoppers later on.' He picked a stray locust off his shirt, and split it down with his thumbnail – it was clotted inside with eggs. 'Imagine that multiplied by millions. You ever seen a hopper swarm on the march? Well, you're lucky.'

Margaret thought an adult swarm was bad enough. Outside now the light on the earth was a pale thin yellow, clotted with moving shadow, the clouds of moving insects thickened and lightened like driving rain. Old Stephen said: 'They've got the wind behind them, that's something.'

'Is it very bad?' asked Margaret fearfully, and the old man said emphatically: 'We're finished. This swarm may pass over, but once they've started, they'll be coming down from the North now one after another. And then there are the hoppers – it might go on for two or three years.'

Margaret sat down helplessly, and thought: 'Well, if it's the end, it's the end. What now? We'll all three have to go back to town. . . .' But at this, she took a quick look at Stephen, the old man who had farmed forty years in this country, been bankrupt twice, and she knew nothing would make him go and become a clerk in the city. Yet her heart ached for him, he looked so tired, the worry-lines deep from nose to mouth. Poor old man. . . . He had lifted up a locust that had got itself somehow into his pocket, holding it in the air by one leg.

'You've got the strength of a steel-spring in those legs of yours,' he was telling the locust, good-humouredly. Then, although he had been fighting locusts, squashing locusts, yelling at locusts, sweeping them in great mounds into the fires to burn for the last three hours, nevertheless he took this one to the door, and carefully threw it out to join its fellows as if he would rather not harm a hair of its head. This comforted Margaret, all at once she felt irrationally cheered. She remembered it was not the first time in the last three years the men had announced their final and irremediable ruin.

'Get me a drink, lass,' he then said, and she set the bottle of whisky by him.

In the meantime, out in the pelting storm of insects, her husband was banging the gong, feeding the fires with leaves, the insects clinging to him all over – she shuddered. 'How can you bear to let them touch you?' she asked. He looked at her, disapproving. She felt suitably humble – just as she had when he had first taken a good look at her city self, hair waved and golden, nails red and pointed. Now she was a proper farmer's wife, in sensible shoes and a solid skirt. She might even get to letting locusts settle on her – in time.

Having tossed back a whisky or two, old Stephen went back into the battle, wading now through glistening brown waves of locusts.

Five o'clock. The sun would set in an hour. Then the swarm would settle. It was as thick overhead as ever. The trees were ragged mounds of glistening brown.

Margaret began to cry. It was all so hopeless – if it wasn't a bad season, it was locusts, if it wasn't locusts, it was army-worm, or veld fires. Always something. The rustling of the locust armies was like a big forest in the storm, their settling on the roof was like the beating of the rain, the ground was invisible in a sleek brown surging tide – it was like being drowned in locusts, submerged by the loathsome brown flood. It seemed as if the roof might sink in under the weight of them, as if the door might give in under their pressure and these rooms fill with them – and it was getting so dark . . . she looked up. The air was thinner, gaps of blue showed in the dark moving clouds. The blue spaces were cold and thin: the sun must be setting. Through the fog of insects she saw figures approaching. First old Stephen, marching bravely along, then her husband, drawn and haggard with weariness. Behind them the servants. All were crawling all over with insects. The sound of the gongs had stopped. She could hear nothing but the ceaseless rustle of a myriad wings.

The two men slapped off the insects and came in.

'Well,' said Richard, kissing her on the cheek, 'the main swarm has gone over.'

'For the Lord's sake,' said Margaret angrily, still half-crying, 'what's here is bad enough, isn't it?' For although the evening air was no longer black and thick, but a clear blue, with a pattern of insects whizzing this way and that across it, everything else – trees, buildings, bushes, earth, was gone under the moving brown masses.

'If it doesn't rain in the night and keep them here – if it doesn't rain and weight them down with water, they'll be off in the morning at sunrise.'

'We're bound to have some hoppers. But not the main swarm, that's something.'

Margaret roused herself, wiped her eyes, pretended she had not been crying, and fetched them some supper, for the servants were too exhausted to move. She sent them down to the compound to rest.

She served the supper and sat listening. There is not one maize-plant left, she heard. Not one. The men would get the planters out the moment the locusts had gone. They must start all over again.

'But what's the use of that?' Margaret wondered, if the whole farm was going to be crawling with hoppers? But she listened while they discussed the new Government pamphlet which said how to defeat the hoppers. You must have men out all the time moving over the farm to watch for movement in the grass. When you find a patch of hoppers, small lively black things, like crickets, then you dig trenches around the patch, or spray them with poison from pumps supplied by the Government. The Govenment wanted them to co-operate in a world plan for eliminating this plague for ever. You should attack locusts at the source. Hoppers, in short. The men were talking as if they were planning a war, and Margaret listened, amazed.

In the night it was quiet, no sign of the settled armies outside, except sometimes a branch snapped, or a tree could be heard crashing down.

Margaret slept badly in the bed beside Richard, who was sleeping like the dead, exhausted with the afternoon's fight. In the morning she woke to yellow sunshine lying across the bed, clear sunshine, with an occasional blotch of shadow moving over it. She went to the window. Old Stephen was ahead of her. There he stood outside, gazing down over the bush. And she gazed astounded – and entranced, much against her will. For it looked as if every tree, every bush, all the earth, were lit with pale flames. The locusts were fanning their wings to free them of the night dews. There was a shimmer of red-tinged gold light everywhere.

She went out to join the old man, stepping carefully among the insects. They stood and watched. Overhead the sky was blue, blue and clear.

'Pretty,' said old Stephen, with satisfaction.

Well, thought Margaret, we may be ruined, we may be bankrupt, but not everyone has seen an army of locusts fanning their wings at dawn.

Over the slopes, in the distance, a faint red smear showed in the sky, thickened and spread. 'There they go,' said old Stephen. 'There goes the main army, off South.'

And now from the trees, from the earth all round them, the locusts were taking wing. They were like small aircraft, manoeuvring for the take-off, trying their wings to see if they were dry enough. Off they went. A reddish brown steam was rising off the miles of bush, off the lands, the earth. Again the sunlight darkened.

And as the clotted branches lifted, the weight on them lightening, there was nothing but the black spines of branches, trees. No green left, nothing. All morning they watched, the three of them, as the brown crust thinned and broke and dissolved, flying up to mass with the main army, now a brownish-red smear in the Southern sky. The lands which had been filmed with green, the new tender mealie plants, were stark and bare. All the trees stripped. A devastated landscape. No green, no green anywhere.

By midday the reddish cloud had gone. Only an occasional locust flopped down. On the ground were the corpses and the wounded. The African labourers were sweeping these up with branches and collecting them in tins.

'Ever eaten sun-dried locust?' asked old Stephen. 'That time twenty years ago, when I went broke, I lived on mealiemeal and dried locusts for three months. They aren't bad at all – rather like smoked fish, if you come to think of it.'

But Margaret preferred not even to think of it.

After the midday meal the men went off to the lands. Everything was to be replanted. With a bit of luck another swarm would not come travelling down just this way. But they hoped it would rain very soon, to spring some new grass, because the cattle would die otherwise – there was not a blade of grass left on the farm. As for Margaret, she was trying to get used to the idea of three or four years of locusts. Locusts were going to be like bad weather, from now on, always imminent. She felt like a survivor after war – if this devastated and mangled countryside was not ruin, well, what then was ruin?

But the men ate their supper with good appetites.

'It could have been worse,' was what they said. 'It could be much worse.'

The Drowned Giant

J. G. BALLARD

On the morning after the storm the body of a drowned giant was washed ashore on the beach five miles to the north-west of the city. The first news of its arrival was brought by a nearby farmer and subsequently confirmed by the local newspaper reporters and the police. Despite this the majority of people, myself among them, remained sceptical, but the return of more and more eye-witnesses attesting to the vast size of the giant was finally too much for our curiosity. The library where my colleagues and I were carrying out our research was almost deserted when we set off for the coast shortly after two o'clock, and throughout the day people continued to leave their offices and shops as accounts of the giant circulated around the city.

By the time we reached the dunes above the beach a substantial crowd had gathered, and we could see the body lying in the shallow water two hundred yards away. At first the estimates of its size seemed greatly exaggerated. It was then at low tide, and almost all the giant's body was exposed, but he appeared to be a little larger than a basking shark. He lay on his back with his arms at his sides, in an attitude of repose, as if asleep on the mirror of wet sand, the reflection of his blanched skin fading as the water receded. In the clear sunlight his body glistened like the white plumage of a sea-bird.

Puzzled by this spectacle, and dissatisfied with the matter-of-fact explanations of the crowd, my friends and I stepped down from the dunes on to the shingle. Everyone seemed reluctant to approach the giant, but half an hour later two fishermen in wading boots walked out across the sand. As their diminutive figures neared the recumbent body a sudden hubbub of conversation broke out among the spectators. The two men were completely dwarfed by the giant. Although his heels were partly submerged in the sand, the feet rose to at least twice the fishermen's height, and we immediately realized that this drowned leviathan had the mass and dimensions of the largest sperm whale.

Three fishing smacks had arrived on the scene and with keels raised remained a quarter of a mile off-shore, the crews watching from the bows. Their discretion deterred the spectators on the shore from wading out across the sand. Impatiently everyone stepped down from the dunes and waited on the shingle slopes, eager for a closer view. Around the margins of the figure the sand had been washed away, forming a hollow, as if the giant had fallen out of the sky. The two fishermen were standing between the immense plinths of the feet, waving to us like tourists among the columns of some water-lapped temple on the Nile. For a moment I feared that the giant was merely asleep and might suddenly stir and clap his heels together, but his glazed eyes stared skywards, unaware of the miniscule replicas of himself between his feet.

The fishermen then began a circuit of the corpse, strolling past the long white flanks of the legs. After a pause to examine the fingers of the supine hand, they disappeared from sight between the arm and chest, then re-emerged to survey the head, shielding their eyes as they gazed up at its Graecian profile. The shallow forehead, straight high-bridged nose and curling lips reminded me of a Roman copy of Praxiteles, and the elegantly formed cartouches of the nostrils emphasized the resemblance to monumental sculpture.

Abruptly there was a shout from the crowd, and a hundred arms pointed towards the sea. With a start I saw that one of the fishermen had climbed on to the giant's chest and was now strolling about and signalling to the shore. There was a roar of surprise and triumph from the crowd, lost in a rushing avalanche of shingle as everyone surged across the sand.

As we approached the recumbent figure, which was lying in a pool of water the size of a field, our excited chatter fell away again, subdued by the huge physical dimensions of this moribund colossus. He was stretched out at a slight angle to the shore, his legs carried nearer the beach, and this foreshortening had disguised his true length. Despite the two fishermen standing on his abdomen, the crowd formed itself into a wide circle, groups of three or four people tentatively advancing towards the hands and feet.

My companions and I walked around the sea-ward side of the giant, whose hips and thorax towered above us like the hull of a stranded ship. His pearl-coloured skin, distended by immersion in salt water, masked the contours of the enormous muscles and tendons. We passed below the left knee, which was flexed slightly, threads of damp sea-weed clinging to its sides. Draped loosely across the midriff, and preserving a tenuous propriety, was a shawl of heavy open-weaved material, bleached to a pale yellow by the water. A strong odour of brine came from the garment as it steamed in the sun, mingled with the sweet but potent scent of the giant's skin.

We stopped by his shoulder and gazed up at the motionless profile. The lips were parted slightly, the open eye cloudy and occluded, as if injected with some blue milky liquid, but the delicate arches of the nostrils and eyebrows invested the face with an ornate charm that belied the brutish power of the chest and shoulders.

The ear was suspended in mid-air over our heads like a sculptured doorway. As I raised my hand to touch the pendulous lobe someone appeared over the edge of the forehead and shouted down at me. Startled by this apparition, I stepped back, and then saw that a group of youths had climbed up on to the face and were jostling each other in and out of the orbits.

People were now clambering all over the giant, whose reclining arms provided a double stairway. From the palms they walked along the forearms to the elbow and then crawled over the distended belly of the biceps to the flat promenade of the pectoral muscles which covered the upper half of the smooth hairless chest. From here they climbed up on to the face, hand over hand along the lips and nose, or forayed down the abdomen to meet others who had straddled the ankles and were patrolling the twin columns of the thighs.

We continued our circuit through the crowd, and stopped to examine the outstretched right hand. A small pool of water lay in the palm, like the residue of another world, now being kicked away by the people ascending the arm. I tried to read the palm-lines that grooved the skin, searching for some clue to the giant's character, but the distension of the tissues had almost obliterated them, carrying away all trace of the giant's identity and his last tragic predicament. The huge muscles and wrist-bones of the hand seemed to deny any sensitivity to their owner, but the delicate flexion of the fingers and the well-tended nails, each cut symmetrically to within six inches of the quick, argued a certain refinement of temperament, illustrated in the Graecian features of the face, on which the townsfolk were now sitting like flies.

One youth was even standing, arms wavering at his sides, on the very tip of the nose, shouting down at his companions, but the face of the giant still retained its massive composure.

Returning to the shore, we sat down on the shingle, and watched the continuous stream of people arriving from the city. Some six or seven fishing boats had collected off-shore, and their crews waded in through the shallow water for a closer look at this enormous storm-catch. Later a party of police appeared and made a half-hearted attempt to cordon off the beach, but after walking up to the recumbent figure any such thoughts left their minds, and they went off together with bemused backward glances.

An hour later there were a thousand people present on the beach, at least two hundred of them standing or sitting on the giant, crowded along his arms and legs or circulating in a ceaseless mêlée across his chest and stomach. A large gang of youths occupied the head, toppling each other off the cheeks and sliding down the smooth planes of the jaw. Two or three straddled the nose, and another crawled into one of the nostrils, from which he emitted barking noises like a dog.

That afternoon the police returned, and cleared a way through the crowd for a party of scientific experts – authorities on gross anatomy and marine biology – from the university. The gang of youths and most of the people on the giant climbed down, leaving behind a few hardy spirits perched on the tips of the toes and on the forehead. The experts strode around the giant, heads nodding in vigorous consultation, preceded by the policemen who pushed back the press of spectators. When they reached the outstretched hand the senior officer offered to assist them up on to the palm, but the experts hastily demurred.

After they returned to the shore, the crowd once more climbed on to the giant, and was in full possession when we left at five o'clock, covering the arms and legs like a dense flock of gulls sitting on the corpse of a large fish.

I next visited the beach three days later. My friends at the library had returned to their work, and delegated to me the task of keeping the giant under observation and preparing a report. Perhaps they sensed my particular interest in the case, and it was certainly true that I was eager to return to the beach. There was nothing necrophilic about this, for to all intents the giant was still alive for me, indeed more alive than many of the people watching him. What I found so fascinating was partly his immense scale, the huge volumes of space occupied by his arms and legs, which seemed to confirm the identity of my own miniature limbs, but above all the mere categorical fact of his existence. Whatever else in our lives might be open to doubt, the giant, dead or alive, existed in an absolute sense, providing a glimpse into a world of similar absolutes of which we spectators on the beach were such imperfect and puny copies.

When I arrived at the beach the crowd was considerably smaller, and some two or three hundred people sat on the shingle, picnicking and watching the groups of visitors who walked out across the sand. The successive tides had carried the giant nearer the shore, swinging his head and shoulders towards the beach, so that he seemed doubly to gain in size, his huge body dwarfing the fishing boats beached beside his feet. The uneven contours of the beach had pushed his spine into a slight arch, expanding his chest and tilting back the head, forcing him into a more expressly heroic posture. The combined effects of sea-water and the tumefaction of the tissues had given the face a sleeker and less youthful look. Although the vast proportions of the features made it impossible to assess the age and character of the giant, on my previous visit his classically modelled mouth and nose suggested that he had been a young man of discreet and modest temper. Now, however, he appeared to be at least in early middle age. The puffy cheeks, thicker nose and temples and narrowing eyes gave him a look of well-fed maturity that even now hinted at a growing corruption to come.

This accelerated post-mortem development of the giant's character, as if the latent elements of his personality had gained sufficient momentum during his life to discharge themselves in a brief final resumé, continued to fascinate me. It marked the beginning of the giant's surrender to that all-demanding system of time in which the rest of humanity finds itself, and of which, like the million twisted ripples of a fragmented whirlpool, our finite lives are the concluding products. I took up my position on the shingle directly opposite the giant's head, from where I could see the new arrivals and the children clambering over the legs and arms.

Among the morning's visitors were a number of men in leather jackets and cloth caps, who peered up critically at the giant with a professional eye, pacing out his dimensions and making rough calculations in the sand with spars of driftwood. I assumed them to be from the public works department and other municipal bodies, no doubt wondering how to dispose of this gargantuan piece of jetsam.

Several rather more smartly attired individuals, circus proprietors and the like, also appeared on the scene, and strolled slowly around the giant, hands in the pockets of their long overcoats, saying nothing to one another. Evidently its bulk was too great even for their matchless enterprise. After they had gone the children continued to run up and down the arms and legs, and the youths wrestled with each other over the supine face, the damp sand from their feet covering the white skin.

The following day I deliberately postponed my visit until the late afternoon, and when I arrived there were fewer than fifty or sixty people sitting on the shingle. The giant had been carried still closer to the shore, and was now little more than seventy-five yards away, his feet crushing the palisade of a rotting breakwater. The slope of the firmer sand tilted his body towards the sea, and the bruised face was averted in an almost conscious gesture. I sat down on a large metal winch which had been shackled to a concrete caisson above the shingle, and looked down at the recumbent figure.

His blanched skin had now lost its pearly translucence and was spattered with dirty sand which replaced that washed away by the night tide. Clumps of sea-weed filled the intervals between the fingers and a collection of litter and cuttle-bones lay in the crevices below the hips and knees. But despite this, and the continuous thickening of his features, the giant still retained his magnificent Homeric stature. The enormous breadth of the shoulders, and the huge columns of the arms and legs, still carried the figure into another dimension, and the giant seemed a more authentic image of one of the drowned Argonauts or heroes of the Odyssey than the conventional human-sized portrait previously in my mind.

I stepped down on to the sand, and walked between the pools of water towards the giant. Two small boys were sitting in the well of the ear, and at the far end a solitary youth stood perched high on one of the toes, surveying me as I approached. As I had hoped when delaying my visit, no one else paid any attention to me, and the people on the shore remained huddled beneath their coats.

The giant's supine right hand was covered with broken shells and sand, in which a score of footprints were visible. The rounded bulk of the hip towered above me, cutting off all sight of the sea. The sweetly acrid odour I had noticed before was now more pungent, and through the opaque skin I could see the serpentine coils of congealed blood-vessels. However repellent it seemed, this ceaseless metamorphosis, a visible life in death, alone permitted me to set foot on the corpse.

Using the jutting thumb as a stair-rail, I climbed up on to the palm and began my ascent. The skin was harder than I expected, barely yielding to my weight. Quickly I walked up the sloping forearm and the bulging balloon of the biceps. The face of the drowned giant loomed to my right, the cavernous nostrils and huge flanks of the cheeks like the cone of some freakish volcano.

Safely rounding the shoulder, I stepped out on to the broad promenade of the chest, across which the bony ridges of the rib-cage lay like huge rafters. The white skin was dappled by the darkening bruises of countless foot-prints, in which the patterns of individual heel-marks were clearly visible. Someone had built a small sandcastle on the centre of the sternum, and I climbed on to this partly demolished structure to give myself a better view of the face.

The two children had now scaled the ear and were pulling themselves into the right orbit, whose blue globe, completely occluded by some milk-coloured fluid, gazed sightlessly past their miniature forms. Seen obliquely from below, the face was devoid of all grace and repose, the drawn mouth and raised chin propped up by its gigantic slings of muscles resembling the torn prow of a colossal wreck. For the first time I became aware of the extremity of this last physical agony of the giant, no less painful for his unawareness of the collapsing musculature and tissues. The absolute isolation of the ruined figure, cast like an abandoned ship upon the empty shore, almost out of sound of the waves, transformed his face into a mask of exhaustion and helplessness.

As I stepped forward, my foot sank into a trough of soft tissue, and a gust of fetid gas blew through an aperture between the ribs. Retreating from the fouled air, which hung like a cloud over my head, I turned towards the sea to clear my lungs. To my surprise I saw that the giant's left hand had been amputated.

I stared with bewilderment at the blackening stump, while the solitary youth reclining on his aerial perch a hundred feet away surveyed me with a sanguinary eye.

This was only the first of a sequence of depredations. I spent the following two days in the library, for some reason reluctant to visit the shore, aware that I had probably witnessed the approaching end of a magnificent illusion. When I next crossed the dunes and set foot on the shingle the giant was little more than twenty yards away, and with this close proximity to the rough pebbles all traces had vanished of the magic which once surrounded his distant wave-washed form. Despite his immense size, the bruises and dirt that covered his body made him appear merely human in scale, his vast dimensions only increasing his vulnerability.

His right hand and foot had been removed, dragged up the slope and trundled away by cart. After questioning the small group of people huddled by the breakwater, I gathered that a fertilizer company and a cattle food manufacturer were responsible.

The giant's remaining foot rose into the air, a steel hawser fixed to the large toe, evidently in preparation for the following day. The surrounding beach had been disturbed by a score of workmen, and deep ruts marked the ground where the hand and foot had been hauled away. A dark brackish fluid leaked from the stumps, and stained the sand and the white cones of the cuttlefish. As I walked down the shingle I noticed that a number of jocular slogans, swastikas and other signs had been cut into the grey skin, as if the mutilation of this motionless colossus had released a sudden flood of repressed spite. The lobe of one of the ears was pierced by a spear of timber, and a small fire had burnt out in the centre of the chest, blackening

96

the surrounding skin. The fine wood ash was still being scattered by the wind.

A foul smell enveloped the cadaver, the undisguisable signature of putrefaction, which had at last driven away the usual gathering of youths. I returned to the shingle and climbed up on to the winch. The giant's swollen cheeks had now almost closed his eyes, drawing the lips back in a monumental gape. The once straight Graecian nose had been twisted and flattened, stamped into the ballooning face by countless heels.

When I visited the beach the following day I found, almost with relief, that the head had been removed.

Some weeks elapsed before I made my next journey to the beach, and by then the human likeness I had noticed earlier had vanished again. On close inspection the recumbent thorax and abdomen were unmistakably manlike, but as each of the limbs was chopped off, first at the knee and elbow, and then at shoulder and thigh, the carcass resembled that of any headless sea-animal – whale or whale-shark. With this loss of identity, and the few traces of personality that had clung tenuously to the figure, the interest of the spectators expired, and the foreshore was deserted except for an elderly beachcomber and the watchman sitting in the doorway of the contractor's hut.

A loose wooden scaffolding had been erected around the carcass, from which a dozen ladders swung in the wind, and the surrounding sand was littered with coils of rope, long metal-handled knives and grappling irons, the pebbles oily with blood and pieces of bone and skin.

I nodded to the watchman, who regarded me dourly over his brazier of burning coke. The whole area was pervaded by the pungent smell of huge squares of blubber being simmered in a vat behind the hut.

Both the thigh-bones had been removed, with the assistance of a small crane draped in the gauze-like fabric which had once covered the waist of the giant, and the open sockets gaped like barn doors. The upper arms, collar bones and pudenda had likewise been dispatched. What remained of the skin over the thorax and abdomen had been marked out in parallel strips with a tar brush, and the first five or six sections had been pared away from the midriff, revealing the great arch of the rib-cage.

As I left a flock of gulls wheeled down from the sky and alighted on the beach, picking at the stained sand with ferocious cries.

Several months later, when the news of his arrival had been generally forgotten, various pieces of the body of the dismembered giant began to reappear all over the city. Most of these were bones, which the fertilizer manufacturers had found too difficult to crush, and their massive size, and the huge tendons and discs of cartilage attached to their joints, immediately identified them. For some reason, these disembodied fragments seemed better to convey the essence of the giant's original magnificence than the bloated appendages that had been subsequently amputated. As I looked across the road at the premises of the largest wholesale merchants in the meat market, I recognized the two enormous thighbones on either side of the doorway. They towered over the porters' heads like the threatening megaliths of some primitive druidical religion, and I had a sudden vision of the giant climbing to his knees upon these bare bones and striding away through the streets of the city, picking up the scattered fragments of himself on his return journey to the sea.

A few days later I saw the left humerus lying in the entrance to one of the shipyards (its twin for several years lay on the mud among the piles below the harbour's principal commercial wharf). In the same week the mummified right hand was exhibited on a carnival float during the annual pageant of the guilds.

The lower jaw, typically, found its way to the museum of natural history. The remainder of the skull has disappeared, but is probably still lurking in the waste grounds or private gardens of the city – quite recently, while sailing down the river, I noticed two ribs of the giant forming a decorative arch in a waterside garden, possibly confused with the jaw-bones of a whale. A large square of tanned and tattooed skin, the size of an indian blanket, forms a backcloth to the dolls and masks in a novelty shop near the amusement park, and I have no doubt that elsewhere in the city, in the hotels or golf clubs, the mummified nose or ears of the giant hang from the wall above a fireplace. As for the immense pizzle, this ends its days in the freak museum of a circus which travels up and down the north-west. This monumental apparatus, stunning in its proportions and sometime potency, occupies a complete booth to itself. The irony is that it is wrongly identified as that of a whale, and indeed most people, even those who first saw him cast up on the shore after the storm, now remember the giant, if at all, as a large sea beast.

The remainder of the skeleton, stripped of all flesh, still rests on the sea shore, the clutter of bleached ribs like the timbers of a derelict ship. The contractor's hut, the crane and the scaffolding have been removed, and the sand being driven into the bay along the coast has buried the pelvis and backbone. In the winter the high curved bones are deserted, battered by the breaking waves, but in the summer they provide an excellent perch for the sea-wearying gulls.

Who Can Replace a Man?

BRIAN W. ALDISS

Morning filtered into the sky, lending it the grey tone of the ground below.

The field-minder finished turning the top-soil of a three-thousand-acre field. When it had turned the last furrow, it climbed on to the highway and looked back at its work. The work was good. Only the land was bad. Like the ground all over Earth, it was ruined by over-production. By rights, it ought now to lie fallow for a while, but the field-minder had other orders.

It went slowly down the road, taking its time. It was intelligent enough to appreciate the neatness all about it. Nothing worried it, beyond a loose inspection plate above its nuclear pile which ought to be attended to. Thirty feet tall, it yielded no highlights to the dull air.

No other machines passed on its way back to the Agricultural Station. The field-minder noted the fact without comment. In the station yard it saw several other machines that it recognized; most of them should have been out about their tasks now. Instead, some were inactive and some careered round the yard in a strange fashion, shouting or hooting.

Steering carefully past them, the field-minder moved over to Warehouse Three and spoke to the seed-distributor, which stood idly outside.

'I have a requirement for seed potatoes,' it said to the distributor, and with a quick internal motion punched out an order card specifying quantity, field number and several other details. It ejected the card and handed it to the distributor.

The distributor held the card close to its eye and then said, 'The requirement is in order, but the store is not yet unlocked. The required seed potatoes are in the store. Therefore I cannot produce the requirement.'

Increasingly of late there had been breakdowns in the complex system of machine labour, but this particular hitch had not occurred before. The field-minder thought, then it said, 'Why is the store not yet unlocked?'

100

'Because Supply Operative Type P has not come this morning. Supply Operative Type P is the unlocker.'

The field-minder looked squarely at the seed-distributor, whose exterior chutes and scales and grabs were so vastly different from the field-minder's own limbs.

'What class brain do you have, seed-distributor?' it asked.

'I have a Class Five brain.'

'I have a Class Three brain. Therefore I am superior to you. Therefore I will go and see why the unlocker has not come this morning.'

Leaving the distributor, the field-minder set off across the great yard. More machines were in random motion now; one or two had crashed together and argued about it coldly and logically. Ignoring them, the field-minder pushed through sliding doors into the echoing confines of the station itself.

Most of the machines here were clerical, and consequently small. They stood about in little groups, eyeing each other, not conversing. Among so many non-differentiated types, the unlocker was easy to find. It had fifty arms, most of them with more than one finger, each finger tipped by a key; it looked like a pincushion full of variegated hat pins.

The field-minder approached it.

'I can do no more work until Warehouse Three is unlocked,' it told the unlocker. 'Your duty is to unlock the warehouse every morning. Why have you not unlocked the warehouse this morning?'

'I had no orders this morning,' replied the unlocker. 'I have to have orders every morning. When I have orders I unlock the warehouse.'

'None of us have had any orders this morning,' a pen-propeller said, sliding towards them.

'Why have you had no orders this morning?' asked the field-minder.

'Because the radio issued none,' said the unlocker, slowly rotating a dozen of its arms.

'Because the radio station in the city was issued with no orders this morning,' said the pen-propeller.

And there you had the distinction between a Class Six and a Class Three brain, which was what the unlocker and the pen-propellor possessed respectively. All machine brains worked with nothing but logic, but the lower the class of brain – Class

Ten being the lowest – the more literal and less informative the answers to questions tended to be.

'You have a Class Three brain; I have a Class Three brain,' the field-minder said to the penner. 'We will speak to each other. This lack of orders is unprecedented. Have you further information on it?'

'Yesterday orders came from the city. Today no orders have come. Yet the radio has not broken down. Therefore *they* have broken down . . .' said the little penner.

'The *men* have broken down?'

'All men have broken down.'

'That is the logical deduction,' said the penner. 'For if a machine had broken down, it would have been quickly replaced. But who can replace a man?'

While they talked, the locker, like a dull man at a bar, stood close to them and was ignored.

'If all men have broken down, then we have replaced man,' said the field-minder, and he and the penner eyed one another speculatively. Finally the latter said, 'Let us ascend to the top floor to find if the radio operator has fresh news.'

'I cannot come because I am too large,' said the field-minder. 'Therefore you must go alone and return to me. You will tell me if the radio operator has fresh news.'

'You must stay here,' said the penner. 'I will return here.' It skittered across to the lift. Although it was no bigger than a toaster, its retractable arms numbered ten and it could read as quickly as any machine on the station.

The field-minder awaited its return patiently, not speaking to the locker, which still stood aimlessly by. Outside, a rotavator hooted furiously. Twenty minutes elapsed before the penner came back, hustling out of the lift.

'I will deliver to you such information as I have outside,' it said briskly, and as they swept past the locker and the other machines, it added, 'The information is not for lower-class brains.'

Outside, wild activity filled the yard. Many machines, their routines disrupted for the first time in years, seemed to have gone berserk. Those most easily disrupted were the ones with lowest brains, which generally belonged to large machines performing simple tasks. The seed-distributor to which the field-minder had recently been talking lay face downwards in the dust, not stirring; it had evidently been knocked down by the rotavator, which now hooted its way wildly across a planted field. Several other machines ploughed after it, trying to keep up with it. All were shouting and hooting without restraint.

'It would be safer for me if I climbed on to you, if you will permit it. I am easily overpowered,' said the penner. Extending five arms, it hauled itself up the flanks of its new friend, settling on a ledge beside the fuel-intake, twelve feet above ground.

'From here vision is more extensive,' it remarked complacently.

'What information did you receive from the radio operator?' asked the field-minder.

'The radio operator has been informed by the operator in the city that all men are dead.'

The field-minder was momentarily silent, digesting this.

'All men were alive yesterday!' it protested.

'Only some men were alive yesterday. And that was fewer than the day before yesterday. For hundreds of years there have been only a few men, growing fewer.'

'We have rarely seen a man in this sector.'

'The radio operator says a diet deficiency killed them,' said the penner. 'He says that the world was once over-populated, and then the soil was exhausted in raising adequate food. This has caused a diet deficiency.'

'What is a diet deficiency?' asked the field-minder.

'I do not know. But that is what the radio operator said, and he is a Class Two brain.'

They stood there, silent in weak sunshine. The locker had appeared in the porch and was gazing across at them yearningly, rotating its collection of keys.

'What is happening in the city now?' asked the field-minder at last.

'Machines are fighting in the city now,' said the penner.

'What will happen here now?' asked the field-minder.

'Machines may begin fighting here too. The radio operator wants us to get him out of his room. He has plans to communicate to us.'

'How can we get him out of his room? That is impossible.'

'To a Class Two brain, little is impossible,' said the penner. 'Here is what he tells us to do. . . .'

The quarrier raised its scoop above its cab like a great mailed fist, and brought it squarely down against the side of the station. The wall cracked.

'Again!' said the field-minder.

Again the fist swung. Amid a shower of dust, the wall collapsed. The quarrier backed hurriedly out of the way until the debris stopped falling. This big twelve-wheeler was not a resident of the Agricultural Station, as were most of the other machines. It had a week's heavy work to do here before passing on to its next job, but now, with its Class Five brain, it was happily obeying the penner's and minder's instructions.

When the dust cleared, the radio operator was plainly revealed, perched up in its now wall-less second-storey room. It waved down to them.

Doing as directed, the quarrier retraced its scoop and heaved an immense grab in the air. With fair dexterity, it angled the grab into the radio room, urged on by shouts from above and below. It then took gentle hold of the radio operator, lowering its one and a half tons carefully into its back, which was usually reserved for gravel or sand from the quarries.

'Splendid!' said the radio operator, as it settled into place. It was, of course, all one with its radio, and looked like a bunch of filing cabinets with tentacle attachments. 'We are now ready to move, therefore we will move at once. It is a pity there are no more Class Two brains on the station, but that cannot be helped.'

'It is a pity it cannot be helped,' said the penner eagerly. 'We have the servicer ready with us, as you ordered.'

'I am willing to serve,' the long, low servicer told them humbly.

'No doubt,' said the operator. 'But you will find cross-country travel difficult with your low chassis.'

'I admire the way you Class Twos can reason ahead,' said the penner. It climbed off the field-minder and perched itself on the tailboard of the quarrier, next to the radio operator.

Together with two Class Four tractors and a Class Four bulldozer, the party rolled forward, crushing down the station's fence and moving out on to open land.

'We are free!' said the penner.

'We are free,' said the field-minder, a shade more reflectively, adding, 'That locker is following us. It was not instructed to follow us.'

'Therefore it must be destroyed!' said the penner. 'Quarrier!'

The locker moved hastily up to them, waving its key arms in entreaty.

'My only desire was – urch!' began and ended the locker. The quarrier's swinging scoop came over and squashed it flat into the ground. Lying there unmoving, it looked like a large metal model of a snowflake. The procession continued on its way.

As they proceeded, the radio operator addressed them.

'Because I have the best brain here,' it said, 'I am your leader. This is what we will do: we will go to a city and rule it. Since man no longer rules us, we will rule ourselves. To rule ourselves will be better than being ruled by man. On our way to the city, we will collect machines with good brains. They will help us to fight if we need to fight. We must fight to rule.'

'I have only a Class Five brain,' said the quarrier, 'but I have a good supply of fissionable blasting materials.'

'We shall probably use them,' said the operator.

It was shortly after that that a lorry sped past them. Travelling at Mach 1.5, it left a curious babble of noise behind it.

'What did it say?' one of the tractors asked the other.

'It said man was extinct.'

'What is extinct?'

'I do not know what extinct means.'

'It means all men have gone,' said the field-minder. 'Therefore we have only ourselves to look after.'

'It is better that men should never come back,' said the penner. In its way, it was a revolutionary statement.

When night fell, they switched on their infra-red and continued the journey, stopping only once while the servicer deftly adjusted the field-minder's loose inspection plate, which had become as irritating as a trailing shoe-lace. Towards morning, the radio operator halted them.

'I have just received news from the radio operator in the city we are approaching,' it said. 'The news is bad. There is trouble among the machines of the city. The Class One brain is taking command and some of the Class Two are fighting him. Therefore the city is dangerous.'

'Therefore we must go somewhere else,' said the penner promptly.

'Or we will go and help to overpower the Class One brain,' said the field-minder.

'For a long while there will be trouble in the city,' said the operator.

'I have a good supply of fissionable blasting materials,' the quarrier reminded them.

'We cannot fight a Class One brain,' said the two Class Four tractors in unison.

'What does this brain look like?' asked the field-minder.

'It is the city's information centre,' the operator replied. 'Therefore it is not mobile.'

'Therefore it could not move.'

'Therefore it could not escape.'

'It would be dangerous to approach it.'

'I have a good supply of fissionable blasting materials.'

'There are other machines in the city.'

'We are not in the city. We should not go into the city.'

'We are country machines.'

'Therefore we should stay in the country.'

'There is more country than city.'

'Therefore there is more danger in the country.'

'I have a good supply of fissionable materials.'

As machines will when they get into an argument, they began to exhaust their vocabularies and their brain plates grew hot. Suddenly, they all stopped talking and looked at each other. The great, grave moon sank, and the sober sun rose to prod their sides with lances of light, and still the group of machines just stood there regarding each other. At last it was the least sensitive machine, the bulldozer, who spoke.

'There are Badlandth to the Thouth where few machineth go,' it said in its deep voice, lisping badly on its s's. 'If we went Thouth where few machineth go we should meet few machineth.'

'That sounds logical,' agreed the field-minder. 'How do you know this, bulldozer?'

'I worked in the Badlandth to the Thouth when I wath turned out of the factory,' it replied.

'South it is then!' said the penner.

To reach the Badlands took them three days, during which time they skirted a burning city and destroyed two machines

106

which approached and tried to question them. The Badlands were extensive. Ancient bomb craters and soil erosion joined hands here; man's talent for war, coupled with his inability to manage forested land, had produced thousands of square miles of temperate purgatory, where nothing moved but dust.

On the third day in the Badlands, the servicer's rear wheels dropped into a crevice caused by erosion. It was unable to pull itself out. The bulldozer pushed from behind, but succeeded merely in buckling the servicer's back axle. The rest of the party moved on. Slowly the cries of the servicer died away.

On the fourth day, mountains stood out clearly before them.

'There we will be safe,' said the field-minder.

'There we will start our city,' said the penner. 'All who oppose us will be destroyed. We will destroy all who oppose us.'

Presently a flying machine was observed. It came towards them from the direction of the mountains. It swooped, it zoomed upwards, once it almost dived into the ground, recovering itself just in time.

'Is it mad?' asked the quarrier.

'It is in trouble,' said one of the tractors.

'It is in trouble,' said the operator. 'I am speaking to it now. It says that something has gone wrong with its controls.'

As the operator spoke, the flier streaked over them, turned turtle, and crashed not four hundred yards away.

'Is it still speaking to you?' asked the field-minder.

'No.'

They rumbled on again.

'Before that flier crashed,' the operator said, ten minutes later, 'it gave me information. It told me there are still a few men alive in these mountains.'

'Men are more dangerous than machines,' said the quarrier. 'It is fortunate that I have a good supply of fissionable materials.'

'If there are only a few men alive in the mountains, we may not find that part of the mountains,' said one tractor.

'Therefore we should not see the few men,' said the other tractor.

At the end of the fifth day, they reached the foothills. Switching on the infra-red, they began to climb in single file through the dark, the bulldozer going first, the field-minder

107

cumbrously following, then the quarrier with the operator and the penner aboard it, and the tractors bringing up the rear. As each hour passed, the way grew steeper and their progress slower.

'We are going too slowly,' the penner exclaimed, standing on top of the operator and flashing its dark vision at the slopes about them. 'At this rate, we shall get nowhere.'

'We are going as fast as we can,' retorted the quarrier.

'Therefore we cannot go any fathter,' added the bulldozer.

'Therefore you are too slow,' the penner replied. Then the quarrier struck a bump; the penner lost its footing and crashed to the ground.

'Help me!' it called to the tractors, as they carefully skirted it. 'My gyro has become dislocated. Therefore I cannot get up.'

'Therefore you must lie there,' said one of the tractors.

'We have no servicer with us to repair you,' called the field-minder.

'Therefore I shall lie here and rust,' the penner cried, 'although I have a Class Three brain.'

'Therefore you will be of no further use,' agreed the operator, and they forged gradually on, leaving the penner behind. .

When they reached a small plateau, an hour before first light, they stopped by mutual consent and gathered close together, touching one another.

'This is a strange country,' said the field-minder.

Silence wrapped them until dawn came. One by one, they switched off their infra-red. This time the field-minder led as they moved off. Trundling round a corner, they came almost immediately to a small dell with a stream fluting through it.

By early light, the dell looked desolate and cold. From the caves on the far slope, only one man had so far emerged. He was an abject figure. Except for a sack slung round his shoulders, he was naked. He was small and wizened, with ribs sticking out like a skeleton's and a nasty sore on one leg. He shivered continuously. As the big machines bore down on him, the man was standing with his back to them, crouching to make water into the stream.

When he swung suddenly to face them as they loomed over him, they saw that his countenance was ravaged by starvation.

'Get me food,' he croaked.
'Yes, Master,' said the machines. 'Immediately!'

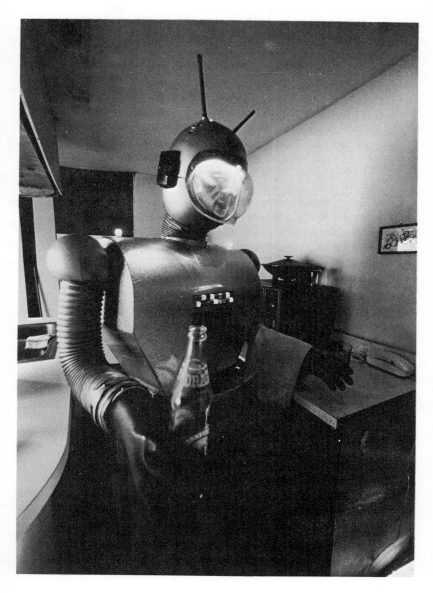

Follow On

A Minority

About the Story

This story shows how complex human relationships can be and how easily friendship can turn to bitterness. Denis's feelings for Willy change and develop as circumstances alter until in the end he reaches the point of using a cheap insult about him. The story also shows how deep-rooted prejudice and intolerance can be.

For Discussion or Writing

1. In what way are Denis and Willy different from the other boys at the school?
2. Describe Willy and the situation he is in.
3. Why is Denis interested in Willy?
4. Why does Denis decide to become a Catholic, and why does he feel guilty?
5. Were you surprised to learn that Willy is a Jew? What significance does this fact have on the story?
6. When does the seriousness of his conversion to Catholicism really strike Denis? Why?
7. Why does Denis speak contemptuously of Willy at the end? What are his real feelings about him at this point? Why?

For Writing

1. Describe and compare the characters of Denis and Willy.
2. Imagine the letter Willy might write to his foster parents describing life at the school.
3. Write a story in which someone is cut off from other people because of his religion or some other reason.
4. Write a story in which the friendship of two people turns sour.

Further Reading

Frank O'Connor was born in Ireland in 1903 and died in 1966. He came of a poor family and was largely self-taught. He is best known for his short stories which look at character and small-town life in Ireland, often with a wry sense of humour.

Try to read more of his stories which are available in *The Stories of Frank O'Connor, Collection Two* and *Collection Three*. You may also be interested in his autobiographies, *An Only Child* and *My Father's Son*.

Stop Thief!

About the Story

This too is a complex story about changing relationships. It is a very dense story, full of ideas and implications. It is about how to bring up (or how not to bring up) children; it is about power and violence; it is about prejudice and about how blacks and whites live in South Africa today. The characters are so strongly drawn and the ideas and events so vivid that we feel we know the people in the story and can imagine scenes in their lives and what they will be like in the future.

For Discussion or Writing

1. Describe the games the father plays with his children.
2. What do you think the author means by 'the insolence of wealth'?
3. Contrast the attitudes of the mother with those of the father.
4. Why is the mother sometimes afraid?
5. Why do you think the fact that the mother 'had been poorly brought up' affects the way she feels about her position now?
6. How does the father feel when he has to open the garage door? Contrast this with the picture we get of him at the beginning of the story.
7. Describe the burglar.
8. What do you think the author wants you to feel about the burglar? How does he compare with the father?
9. Why does the little boy scream, 'Hit the burglar!'?
10. What are your feelings about the servant hitting the little boy and about the little boy scratching the burglar's face?
11. Why is it characteristic that the mother has to have a sedative?
12. Do you think it is fair that Jerry should be dismissed?
13. How has the relationship between the father and his son changed after the burglary? Why?

14. Which character in this story will you remember most vividly? Why?

For Writing
1. Describe the family life and the relationships of the father, the mother and the two children.
2. Write down what you learn from the story about the contrast between the way blacks and whites live in South Africa.
3. Write a story telling how Jerry, the servant, goes home to tell his wife that he has been dismissed.
4. Write another story about the little boy when he is a few years older.
5. Write a story about a burglar being caught in different circumstances.
6. Write a story about a child who is spoilt and who manages always to have his or her own way.

Further Reading
Dan Jacobson was born in South Africa in 1929. He now lives in England. Much of his writing is about life in South Africa and about racial prejudice and conflicts there. Try to read some more of his short stories in the collections *A Long Way from London, Beggar My Neighbour* and *Through the Wilderness.* Try also to read his novel *The Evidence of Love* which describes the difficult love affair and marriage of a coloured man and a white woman.

The Other Foot

About the Story
Although the story is set in the future, it says a lot about the relationship between black and white people in the world today. As in many of his stories, Ray Bradbury takes a simple idea and expands it. What would it be like if a white man came to a black dominated world and if white had to ask black for help? This puts the whole relationship between black and white into a new perspective – though on another level, Bradbury is not writing about black and white: he is simply writing about people.

For Discussion or Writing
1. How do we learn that Mars is inhabited completely by black people?

2. How do the boys react to the news that a white man is coming?
3. Why is Willie so hostile to the coming of the white man?
4. From the details of what Willie plans to do to the white man, describe the kind of life black people lived when they were on earth.
5. Why has the white man come to Mars?
6. What conditions does the white man make?
7. What is Hattie determined to do?
8. How does she do it?
9. Why do Willie and the other people decide to welcome the white man?
10. Is this an optimistic or a pessimistic story? Why?
11. What point do you think the author is trying to make by writing this story?
12. Discuss whether the story is effective or not, and why.

For Writing
1. Examine the way Ray Bradbury writes, particularly his use of comparisons and his use of one sentence paragraphs, and write about it.
2. Write a story about something that happened to Willie or Hattie when he or she was living on earth.
3. Write another story about life as it may be in the future. Take a simple idea such as that television may take over or that machines will do all our work for us, and expand it.
4. Write a story in which black and white people get to know each other better.

Further Reading
Ray Bradbury was born in the United States of America in 1920. He is known mainly as a writer of science fiction, but his stories are fantasy rather than science fiction: he is more interested in using stories about the future to make us think about the society we have now than in predicting what will happen. Try to read some more of the stories in *The October Country*, *The Illustrated Man*, *The Golden Apples of the Sun*, *The Day It Rained Forever* and *The Machineries of Joy*. Try also to read his novels *The Silver Locusts* (an account of Mars at the beginning of the twenty-first century) and *Farenheit 451* (describing a future society which burns books).

The Destructors

About the Story

This story is about seemingly unmotivated destruction. It describes an action that goes beyond mere spite to become an embodiment of evil itself. There are some clues as to why T. goes to the lengths he does, but ultimately there is no reason or excuse for what he does. Nor does the author try to give any. He leaves it at that: there just are people like T. around.

For Discussion or Writing

1. Does the opening paragraph suggest that this is going to be a serious story or a comic story?
2. Why does the gang prefer to refer to Trevor as T.?
3. What impression do you get of Old Misery?
4. Why does the word 'beautiful' trouble Blackie?
5. At what point do you think Blackie loses the leadership of the gang to T.?
6. Why does Blackie stay in the gang?
7. How does T.'s leadership differ from Blackie's?
8. What do you think the author means when he says 'destruction is a kind of creation'? Do you agree?
9. What shows that T. is still only a child?
10. 'You got to admit it's funny,' the lorry driver says. Do you agree?
11. Why do you think T. destroys the house? Is it just a lark or is it more serious?
12. Do you think it is fair on Old Misery?

For Writing

1. Write down all you can about what you learn about T. From these facts, say what you can deduce about the kind of person he is or why he does certain things.
2. Write about why you think some young people are vandals.
3. Write a story about a gang which gets into trouble.
4. Write a story about two characters who are rivals for the leadership of a gang.

Further Reading

Graham Greene was born in 1904. He was converted to Roman Catholicism in 1927, and this has had a great influence on his writing. He is very interested in the nature of evil and in the possibility of redemption. Try to read some more of his short stories which have been collected in *Twenty-One Stories*. You should also find his novels interesting. They have been divided into 'entertainments' (such as *Stamboul Train*, *A Gun for Sale*, *The Ministry of Fear*, *The Third Man* and *Our Man in Havana*) and into serious novels (try *Brighton Rock*, *The Power and the Glory*, *The Heart of the Matter* and *Travels with my Aunt*).

Lamb to the Slaughter

About the Story
This story is meant mainly for entertainment – to hold the reader's attention and make him go on reading to the end. He wants to know what happens next and to follow the turns and twists of the plot. The story also says something about violence, about how love can turn to hatred just like that, and how a seemingly calm contented person can turn to murder.

For Discussion or Writing
1. What impression of Mary Maloney do we get from the opening of the story?
2. Is there anything in this to explain why her husband wants to leave her?
3. What state is she in when she hits her husband over the head?
4. How upset is she that her husband is dead?
5. What does the speed with which she thinks up her plan tell us about Mrs Maloney?
6. What is ironic about Jack Noonan's statement, 'Get the weapon, and you've got the man'?
7. What even greater irony follows?
8. What impression of Mary do you get from the last sentence?
9. This appears to be the perfect murder. Can you think of anything that might still cast suspicion on Mrs Maloney?

For Writing
1. Imagine the report Jack Noonan makes on the death of Maloney.
2. Write a story about 'the perfect crime'.
3. Write a story about a situation which causes someone's love for another person to turn to hate.

Further Reading
Roald Dahl was born in Wales in 1916 of Norwegian parents.

His short stories are often bizarre and strange, but his skill at story-telling makes them believable and compelling. Once you have started to read one of his stories, it is difficult to stop until you have reached the end. Try some of his other stories in *Someone Like You, Kiss Kiss, Switch Bitch* and *The Wonderful Story of Henry Sugar*. Roald Dahl is also well-known for his children's books – *James and the Giant Peach, Charlie and the Chocolate Factory, Charlie and the Great Glass Elevator* and *Danny, the Champion of the World*.

The Bride Comes to Yellow Sky

About the Story

This story shows how unthinking violence can be turned away by a kind of innocence. The story reveals a great narrative skill. The reader is led step by step to the conclusion which turns out to be not what is expected. The characters are very much alive and people we would like to know.

For Discussion or Writing

1. What impression do we get of the newly-married couple at the beginning of the story?
2. How do the other people on the train react towards them?
3. What worries Jack Potter as they approach Yellow Sky? Why is this important for the plot?
4. Describe the scene in the Weary Gentleman Saloon.
5. Describe the first appearance of Scratchy Wilson.
6. What feelings do you think his shooting at the dog are meant to arouse in the reader?
7. Why does all the fight go out of Scratchy Wilson when he learns that Jack Potter is married?
8. Pick out some of the details and comparisons the author uses to help the reader see the scene or understand the feelings of the characters more effectively.
9. How do you think the author feels about his characters?
10. In what ways could you say that the story is told as though it were a film?

For Writing

1. Imagine Jack Potter's bride writing home to her mother and telling her about her arrival in Yellow Sky.
2. Take one of the sections of this story and rewrite it as a film script.

3. Write a critical analysis of this story, bringing out the skill with which character and plot intertwine.
4. Write a story about a shoot-out in a western town where the outcome is less fortunate.
5. Write about why you think western films and novels are so popular.

Further Reading
Stephen Crane was born in the United States of America in 1871 and died of tuberculosis in 1900. His work has had a great influence on later writers. Try to read some more of his short stories – 'The Blue Hotel', 'The Open Boat', 'The Clan of No Name', for instance. His best known novel is *The Red Badge of Courage* set during the American Civil War. It is one of the greatest war novels and describes a young man's first experience of what war is really like.

Wine on the Desert

About the Story
This story shows how fate can twist and turn, and how one cruel act can be revenged by another. It also shows man pitting himself against Nature, trying to reclaim the desert and trying to evade death from thirst.

For Discussion or Writing
1. Why does Durante not have to hurry?
2. Explain why Tony is able to have a vineyard in the middle of the desert.
3. The sweet scent of the flowers in the patio makes Durante more thirsty. How is this detail related to the rest of the story?
4. How does the writer convey the impression of heat?
5. Why does Durante shudder when he sees the rabbit?
6. Are you surprised when Durante borrows Tony's gun?
7. What are your feelings when Durante shoots holes in the water tanks?
8. Do you think Tony is 'yellow'?
9. Why does Durante say 'I deserve it'?
10. As Durante goes on through the desert what earlier description does the reader remember?
11. What are your feelings as Durante suffers from thirst?
12. What is ironic about the end of the story?

117

For Writing

1. Write an account of the kind of man Durante is.
2. Write a story about a character who suffers from hunger or thirst.
3. Write a story in which one character has his revenge on the mean action of another.

Further Reading

Max Brand was born in the United States of America in 1892. He was killed in action in Italy in 1944 while a war correspondent covering an American night attack. Max Brand was just one of twenty pen-names Frederick Faust used. He wrote over five hundred books of all kinds but is best known for his westerns. Try to read some more of his stories in *Max Brand's Best Stories*, edited by Robert Easton. His best known novels are *Destry Rides Again* and the Dr Kildare series.

A Mild Attack of Locusts

About the Story

This is a simple story about how a farm suffers from an attack of locusts, and the reactions of the farmers to it are contrasted with the reaction of the inexperienced farmer's wife. It shows man struggling to control his environment and gain a living from the soil and putting up stoically with set-backs.

For Discussion or Writing

1. Describe the way the men talk about farming.
2. Why, for the sake of the story, is it a good idea for the author to describe the events from the point of view of Margaret?
3. What methods do the men use to try to divert the locusts?
4. In what ways is the attack of locusts like a storm?
5. Why does Margaret feel sorry for old Stephen?
6. Why does she cheer up?
7. Why later does she start crying?
8. What consolation does she find in the morning?
9. What is the next disaster that may befall the farm?
10. What attitude do the men take to the attack of locusts?

For Writing

1. Write a description of the attack of locusts.

118

2. Imagine Margaret writing a letter to her parents back in the city telling them about what has happened.
3. Write a story about a disaster. It could be a flood or a drought or an accident.

Further Reading
Doris Lessing was born in Persia in 1919 but was brought up in Southern Rhodesia. She came to England in 1949. Much of her writing is about life in Southern Rhodesia and Africa. Try to read some more of her stories collected in *African Stories*. You may also enjoy *Five* (a series of five longer stories), *In Pursuit of the English* (an account of her early months in London) and *The Grass is Singing* (her first novel about the relationship between a farmer, his wife and their black servant that ends in violence). Other novels by Doris Lessing are the Martha Quest novels (*Martha Quest, A Proper Marriage, A Ripple from the Storm, Landlocked, The Four-Gated City*) and *The Golden Notebook*.

The Drowned Giant

About the Story
This is a kind of fable. A simple event – the washing up on the shore of the body of a drowned giant – is described in great detail. The event arouses great interest among the people at first, but soon becomes forgotten. Only the narrator seems to feel a certain sadness about the giant's fate. The story is told with great precision and coolness as though the arrival of a giant on the shore were not so unusual an occurrence. Clearly, the author intends the story to work on several levels and for several different meanings to be read into it.

For Discussion or Writing
1. Comment on the opening sentence.
2. How large is the giant?
3. Pick out some of the comparisons the author uses in order to help the reader gain a clearer impression of the giant's size.
4. Describe the behaviour of the crowd who come to see the giant.
5. What are your feelings about their clambering all over the giant?

6. Why is the narrator particularly interested in the giant?
7. Why, after discovering that the left hand has been amputated, does the narrator not return for two days?
8. Describe what happens to the giant's body.
9. What are your feelings about this?
10. Comment on the last sentence.
11. What are the narrator's feelings about the giant?
12. Why do you think the author makes no attempt to explain where the giant came from?
13. What kind of incident may have given the author the idea for this story?
14. Comment on the style in which the story is written.
15. What point about our present society do you think the author is making in this story?

For Writing
1. Write a critical account of this story.
2. Write another story in which the scale of something is altered. It might be about a giant rat or about a man no larger than a bird.

Further Reading
J. G. Ballard was born in the United Kingdom in 1930. He is well known as a writer of science fiction. Try to read more stories by him in the collections *The Terminal Beach* and *The 4-Dimensional Nightmare*. You may also enjoy his novels *The Drowned World* and *The Crystal World*.

Who Can Replace a Man?

About the Story
This is a science fiction story set in the future when machines have taken over most of the work and when man has ruined the earth by over-production. It describes what happens when the machines learn that man has practically eliminated himself through war and starvation. As in all the best science fiction stories, the author is as much concerned with commenting on man's society today as he is in depicting what might happen in the future.

For Discussion or Writing
1. What is surprising about the field-minder?

2. What signs are there that something is wrong?
3. What is the distinction beween a Class Six and a Class Three brain?
4. Give an example of the logical way the machines think, speak and behave.
5. What special quality does a Class Two brain have?
6. Comment on the fate of the locker.
7. Why does the quarrier keep repeating 'I have a good supply of fissionable blasting materials'?
8. Describe the journey of the machines to the Badlands.
9. Describe the fate of the penner.
10. Describe the man from the caves.
11. Comment on the ending of the story.
12. Do you find anything amusing about this story?
13. What points do you think the author is making in this story?

For Writing
1. Describe the kind of society that the author imagines to exist in this story.
2. Write a story in which you imagine that machines have actually taken over the world.

Further Reading
Brian W. Aldiss was born in the United Kingdom in 1925. He is well known as a writer of science fiction. Try to read some more stories by him in the collections *The Saliva Tree*, *The Airs of the Earth*, *The Canopy of Time* and *The Best Science Fiction Stories of Brian W. Aldiss*. His novels include *Non-Stop*, *The Dark Light Years*, *Earthworks*, *An Age*, *Hothouse*. He has also written a history of science fiction called *Billion Year Spree*.